No Time For Tears

Lenore McKelvey Puhek

Books by the author

The River's Edge:

Thomas Francis Meagher

and

Elizabeth Townsend Meagher,

Their Love Story

Annie: The Cabin In The Woods

Forever Friends

No Time For Tears

Books are available from iUniverse, internet, website, and bookstores.
Autographed copies can be obtained from the author.
Discounts given for book clubs.

Lenore McKelvey Puhek, P.O. Box 6002, Helena, Mt.
59604.
E-mail: lpuhek@gmail.com.

No Time For Tears

Sequel to Forever Friends

Lenore McKelvey Puhek

iUniverse LLC
Bloomington

No Time For Tears
Sequel to Forever Friends

Graphic Artist book cover design by Ellen McKelvey Murphy copyright 2013.

Certain characters in this work are historical figures, and certain events portrayed did take place. However, this is a work of fiction. All of the other characters, names, and events as well as all places, incidents, organizations, and dialogue in this novel are either the products of the author's imagination or are used fictitiously.

iUniverse books may be ordered through booksellers or by contacting:

iUniverse LLC
1663 Liberty Drive
Bloomington, IN 47403
www.iuniverse.com
1-800-Authors (1-800-288-4677)

Autographed copies may be obtained from the author:
Lenore McKelvey Puhek
P.O. Box 6002
Helena, MT 59604
E-Mail: lpuhek@gmail.com

ISBN: 978-1-4917-0777-7 (sc)
ISBN: 978-1-4917-0779-1 (hc)
ISBN: 978-1-4917-0778-4 (ebk)

Library of Congress Control Number: 2013916557

Printed in the United States of America

iUniverse rev. date: 09/14/2013

Art work: Ellen McKelvey Murphy
Book cover design: Ellen McKelvey Murphy
Photography: Lenore McKelvey Puhek, Ellen McKelvey Murphy and John T. Murphy. Hicks family photos provided by Glenn and Gerri Wilson.

(Some of the older photographs of the Frey family were taken by the author's grandmother, Mary Frey, who developed her own pictures.)

Computer graphics interior design: Ellen McKelvey Murphy.
Computer text assistance: Rylee Quigley
Reader/editor of manuscript: Stevie Erving

CHARACTERS

Dr. Amelia Roberts Martin, M.D.:	From Virginia family, early day female doctor in Helena, Montana Territory.
Mary *Milka* Mutchnik:	Wife of Mr. Mutchnik
Mr. Mutchnik:	Owns the mercantile
Josephine *Josie* Hicks:	Widow of Jeremiah James Hicks. She is the mother of Little Frankie. Later, she married Frank Hicks.
Frankie Hicks:	Toddler. Also Frankie young man.
Frank Hicks:	Virginia farmer. Marries Josie. Homesteads.
Matilda, *Tillie, Tilda* Hicks:	Daughter of Josie and Frank Hicks.
Beulah:	Freed slave from Virginia.
John (Jack) Frey:	Cowboy. Marries Sarah Marie.
Children of Jack and Sarah Marie:	Helen, Celine, Elsie, Gertrude and Nora Bee.
Jackie Severtson:	Grandson raised by Sarah Marie and Jack Frey.
Sarah Marie Frey:	Marries Jack Frey and homesteads near Wolf Creek.
Mrs. Katherine Roberts:	Mother of Amelia and Sarah Marie.
Dr. L. Rodney Pococke, M. D.:	Beloved doctor.

| Mr. James P. Ball: | Black abolitionist and photographer. Known for his photographs of the civil war. |
| The Wong family: | Chinese family members. |

Author's Note: For clarity of the story, I gave several of the characters different names. For example, in real life, Sarah Marie was called "Mary" by her husband, Jack Frey. Josie Hicks was called "Mary" by her family. Mrs. Mutchnik's name was "Mary" but her husband called her "Milka" which is "Mary" in Yugoslavian.

Confusing? Hopefully, only to the author.

Lenore McKelvey Puhek

Dedication

This work is dedicated to all my relatives . . .

past, present and future.

Without them there would be no story to tell.

*There are unwritten chapters in the history of every new
settlement, which no pen will ever write,
but could they be written,
they would tell of many heroines as well as heroes,
women as brave and deserving of credit as those who
landed from the Mayflower.
They have had much to do in "winning the west,"
and a higher civilization has always followed closely in
the footsteps of the woman pioneer.*

*Lucia Darling Park
1839-1905*

Amelia

~1~

Dr. Amelia Martin

Amelia grabbed for the post railing as she stumbled on the uneven, hastily built wooden steps leading to the front door of the abandoned miner's shack.

Well! That's something . . . I can't even see my own two feet anymore. Amelia set down her black medicine bag and wrapped her hands across her blossoming belly. She patted the top of her skirt. *It won't be too many more days and, thankfully, I'll have my baby in my arms for real.*

The front door opened slightly.

"Who's there? Show yourself."

"It's me, Mary. I've come to check on you today."

She watched for the familiar face of Mary Mutchnik, her patient, and now also a dear friend, to appear.

Mary had been seriously injured when a mine explosion near town had rocked the whole valley. The cook-shack's wall where Mary had been working collapsed, pinning her beneath the weight and rubble. The accident, occurring during a warm day in October, caught everyone off guard. Workers dug frantically to free Mrs. Mutchnik. They were able to drag her from the wreckage, but severe damage had occurred to both of her legs, hips, and spine, leaving the aging woman to a permanent life in a make-shift wheelchair.

Amelia realized she was breathing harder than usual, and paused a bit longer.

"I needed some fresh air, Mary, and decided to come to visit you. Amelia brushed at her cloak. She flung it over the porch railing rather than take it inside with her. "Well, you come in this house right now and have a cup of herb tea. It's a good thing to see you today. I was wishing for some company."

Amelia smiled at the warm welcome. "You have any cookies to go with that tea? I'm needing something sweet today myself."

Suddenly, Amelia felt a tug at her waistline. An intense pain grabbed her very being. She had a fleeting thought that she should leave for the clinic, but decided to drink a cup of warm tea. After all, she had many aches and pains and a drizzling rain had started falling. She'd visit until the rain stopped.

"Where is everybody? I had hoped to play with little Frankie this afternoon, too."

Mrs. Mutchnik put some of her oatmeal cookies onto a hand-painted plate and pushed her way from the counter to the wood table in the spacious kitchen.

"You certainly can get around in that wheel chair contraption Mr. Mutchnik had built for you. It's wonderful to see you up from your bed and doing some things. When I came inside, I spotted a knitting project . . . maybe a blanket?" Amelia walked to the side table and picked up the yarn. "Hmm . . . . light baby blue . . . anyone I know going to be wrapping a newborn in a blanket very soon?" She looked at the older woman and was happy to see a twinkle in her greenish brown Irish eyes. A wide smile softened the pain Amelia knew Mary tried to hide from them.

As Amelia was pouring the hot water into china cups brought from the Mutchnik's boarding house in St. Louis, the back door swung open and a whirlwind of a little boy entered into the room. The tyke wobbled across the plank floor to Mary and threw his little arms up for her to grab and pull him into her lap. He patted Mary's cheek, not realizing that Dr. Martin was visiting.

"Look who's here, Frankie, just in time to have a cookie with us." Mary pointed to Amelia. "Can you say hello to Doctor Martin?" She was pulling his little arms out of a knitted sweater.

Frankie just stared with wide open eyes. Then a cute, toothless smile spread out across his puffy cheeks. He shook his head and shut his eyes real tight.

Amelia walked over to the boy. "Oh! You do *too* know me." She reached out and ruffled his light brown curly hair before she helped him down to the floor. She watched him toddle across the plank floor where he climbed up to the kitchen table. Amelia had set out an oatmeal cookie. Frankie began crunching up the cookie, making a mess on the table and the floor beneath the chair.

Amelia couldn't help but stare at the little tyke. Her thoughts drifted. *You look just like your father, you precious baby boy. How I want to hold you and give you kisses and tickle your feet.*

Several opportunities had passed Amelia by to talk to Josie about the teenaged love she had had for Jeremiah. Amelia was sure Josie had no idea that she and Jeremiah even knew each other. Jeremiah had married Josie in St. Louis. Amelia knew she had no right to entertain thoughts of their youthful love back in Virginia.

Amelia had not been able to help Jeremiah medically, and it numbed her body and soul that he died in her clinic after the horrible explosion. She still had nightmares about the sight of him lying on a plank brought into the clinic by two men who witnessed the terrible accident.

Amelia pulled back her hand and reached for her huge belly. Just like Josie, Amelia was a very recent widow. Her baby would be hers alone. She would love him with a true mother's love and long for her beloved. Being married to Dr. Martin had been pure bliss and she loved him unconditionally. *How absurd that he was shot down in the light of day by a deranged patient.*

4

Deciding that she needed a fresh start in life, Amelia convinced her sister, Sarah Marie, and her house maid Beulah, to journey with her into the "Wild West" with the destination of Helena, Montana Territory. She was a passenger on a boat to Ft. Benton that she suspected she was "with child."

To this day, Amelia had not written to tell her mother the news about the blessed event soon to take place. She didn't want her mother and father to worry.

Amelia felt another sharp pain. *My baby might be born in an abandoned miner's shack while in the hospitality of the Mutchnik's.* How foreign is this world compared to what she had left behind. *It is absolutely unbelievable how lives can change in a heartbeat.* Amelia came back to center her attentions on Frankie.

"Where is your Mama? It alarmed Amelia that he was out and about by himself in the rain, even though the store was just a yard to the left of the house.

The Mutchnik Mercantile was a thriving hardware store that carried almost everything the pioneer families needed to go about their daily living in Helena, Montana Territory.

Because the frontier was rapidly expanding after the Civil War had ended, Mr. and Mrs. Mutchnik recognized the opportunity to move with the young couple who had boarded with them in St. Louis. The couple had registered as Josie and James J. Hill, and it wasn't until the group had reached their destination that they revealed their true identities.

Josie and James were both deserters from the Confederate Army. The young man's true name was

Jeremiah J. Hicks from Virginia. He was the son of a farming family. He and Josie were hell bent for Montana Territory where Jeremiah's parents and siblings had already established homestead land in the 1862 Homestead Act.

They had only arrived a few weeks earlier when Jeremiah, also known as James, was killed by a runaway wagon team the day of the horrible explosion. Josie now lived with her son in the Mutchnik household, at their insistence. After all, wasn't she like their very own daughter? She worked in the mercantile store a few hours every day keeping the books, waiting on customers, and sorting what mail that found its' way to the far reaches of Montana Territory. Frankie played and took naps in a sectioned off corner by the big desk where Josie could watch over him and do her work as well.

Josie helped Mrs. Mutchnik with household chores, cooking, cleaning, and nursing the older woman slowly back to health once again. As Amelia watched the interaction between the two women, she realized it was Josie's persistence that brought strength to the mangled legs, giving the older woman hope that she was not doomed to spend her life as a prisoner in her own home.

Having the baby to tend to was a blessing for the three adults. Mr. Mutchnik took it upon himself to be Frankie's stand-in father and the two were inseparable. Every morning, rain or shine, he pushed Frankie in a four-wheeled pram that had handle bars at one end for Mr. Mutchnik to hang on to as he walked over the wood slats for sidewalks. When the weather turned colder and the first snow fell upon the little community, Josie bundled him up tight with a fur hat over his ears. Mrs. Mutchnik had knitted a boy-sized scarf and some mittens that she sewed into his heavy wool coat. Every day Mary said, "You stay bundled up, you hear?" Then she'd pinch a cheek.

"Hello! What brings you out on a day like this?" The back door opened and banged shut behind Josie as she followed her son into the kitchen. Amelia jumped at the low-pitched woman's voice, not having heard her come up on the porch.

"Josie. Hello to you. I was wondering where you were." She smiled at the young woman. "Frankie certainly is walking early, isn't he? It must be a chore to keep up with him once he takes off."

Amelia stood up and stretched her arms high over her head before placing her hands on her hips. "I felt like taking a walk and visit a bit with Mary and Frankie . . . and you."

Amelia straightened her back. She felt another attack coming, this one strong and persistent. Something was changing as panic gripped Amelia. She looked around the room and remembered that Mrs. Mutchnik's bed replaced the parlor furniture off to the right of the kitchen.

"I think I need to rest a minute. Josie, would you help me to the bed, please?"

The two women moved slowly to the bedside and Amelia gingerly lowered herself on top of the straw mattress and quilt.

Amelia pulled Josie down to her. "Josie, I need a favor of you. Run as fast as you can to the clinic and bring Beulah back with you. Tell her to bring her midwife supplies. I think I am about to deliver my firstborn." She shut her eyes very tightly and clenched her teeth. "Would you also go to the clinic and leave a note for my sister, Sarah Marie, telling her where I am?"

Josie looked over at Mary, motioned for her to watch Frankie, then turned and ran out the front door. She noticed Amelia's cloak on the railing and she wrapped it around herself as she started running down the sidewalk. The clinic might as well be a mile away it seemed as she ran pell-mell with her head down, trying to make her way through the now drenching rain.

Oh! God! Please have Beulah be in the clinic, please . . . Josie said a hurried prayer. She almost ran into a wagon team that was crossing the street in front of her.

"Whoa, there, Missy. Where you going in such a hurry?"

Josie looked up into the eyes of John Frey, a local cowboy that most people called "Jack", which he preferred. Without skipping a step she jumped into the wagon box, to sit next to him on the spring bench.

"Get me to the clinic, Mr. Frey. We need help at the Mutchnik house right away."

Jack rapped the horses' hides with the reins and they set off at a fast clip up the rutted dirt hillside road named Broadway Avenue. The clinic was located at the top of the hill, just off one road on Rodney Street.

Thank you Lord for sending me this man . . . *We'll get Beulah to Amelia's side in no time now.*

Josie, sitting next to the driver, for the first time realized she was out of breath. Memories of her own child-birthing in St. Louis flooded her heart, and tears stung her eyes as she remembered that her dead husband was no longer a part of her life. She swiped at her eyes. *Buck up! This is no time for tears. You get Beulah and her medical bag.*

She saw Beulah sweeping the front porch. Josie jumped from the wagon bed before the cowboy had even set the brake. She ran straight into Beulah's arms. "Hurry, Beulah. Dr. Amelia needs you right quick. I think the baby is coming."

She swept past Beulah and found a pencil and a note pad by the door. She quickly scrawled a note for Sarah Marie and propped the paper on top of the doctor's desk, where she was sure the younger sister would find it. She added that Amelia was at the Mutchnik shack about to give birth.

Knowing it would be a while before Josie returned, Mrs. Mutchnik wheeled her way into the kitchen where she dropped a cloth into a bucket of water setting on the edge of the counter. *I must have Mr. Mutchnik bring in water from the well for Beulah. We'll need hot water tonight, and he will have to bring in wood for the stove.*

She wrung out the cloth and returned to Amelia who was beading with perspiration on her forehead and chin. Mary noted that Amelia was restless.

"Here dear. You'll be just fine. Just put this over your eyes." Mrs. Mutchnik spoke with authority but she was quaking. *I went through this with Josie last year, and we did just fine.* Mary tried to stand up but fell back into the chair. *What do I know about birthing? I've never had a child. Oh! What about Frankie? I have to get Mr. Mutchnik home right now.*

"Home" was an abandoned one floor miner's shack, with an outhouse out back, and a well by the kitchen door. But it was spacious enough for them to spend their evenings together. Mary maneuvered the inside floor very well with her wheelchair. Never would she reveal to them how uncomfortable that wheelchair was to sit in, with the straight unbending back and the wood slat seat. Even pillows didn't help much. Mr. Mutchnik was pleased when he drew up the plans for a workman to build the contraption, and it did give her some independence during the day when both Mr. Mutchnik and Josie were at the mercantile building. By summer she would need a ramp covering the back steps and, hopefully, she would have a much better chair that had more maneuverability and comfort in its design.

Work on their new home had come to a halt during the past winter months, but there was hope construction would begin again soon. Supplies were scarce as hen's teeth and workmen were at a premium. But, with the Missouri River cracking free from nature's icy grip, the boats would be loaded in St. Louis, and in another month, Ft. Benton would be the hub of the territory.

Men, held back last winter in the big city, would be anxious for the move west for work. The house building outcome looked favorable, and perhaps the family would be in their own living quarters by that next fall. Mr. Mutchnik would see to it, hiring men as they came off the paddle boats. He had a shack available for men to bunk in and he'd find someone to cook taking Mary's place at that job.

Inside the old shack they had adapted the space to fit their needs: kitchen, pantry, sectioned off areas for bedroom arrangements, and a small welcoming room for the few guests who came by. Most people inquired about Mary at the Mercantile where they visited with Josie and Mr. Mutchnik. A few lady friends from the interdenom-inational church occasionally stopped by, bringing a dinner or a homemade pie. Frankie spent his daytime at the store, and his toys, blocks and wooden wagons were kept available to him in both places.

Mr. Mutchnik had set a pole right next to the front door on the top landing of the porch. He had nailed a school bell to the top and tied a long piece of rope that even Frankie could pull if told to. It was a signal device in case Mary needed him. So far, he had never heard the bell ringing.

What is that clambering? It sounds like it is coming from the house. It IS coming from the porch. What can be wrong? Where is Frankie, Josie?

Mr. Mutchnik grabbed his fur hat to cover his head from the drizzling rain as he ran out the side door of the store. A couple of customers wandering among the aisles were not even aware that he had left the building.

Sarah Marie

~2~

Sarah Marie

Sarah Marie heard the clatter from the wagon as the horses pulled it up the muddy street, stopping at the clinic's door. She walked over to the window in the Fiske house dining room, now her school room, and pulled back the lace curtains. She, her sister Amelia, and Beulah called the Victorian style mansion "home" ever since their arrival in Helena last fall.

That very day Sarah Marie hired on as school teacher to the six Fiske siblings and four other children of Mrs. Fiske's acquaintances. There was no public school in the community and most did not attend any classes at all.

"Children! Children, please be still for just one minute. I'll be right back." Sarah Marie opened the side door of the Fiske house and stepped outside, wishing she had remembered her cloak to toss around her shoulders. The rain had stopped but a fog hung over the valley and the air held a chill. She fixed her eyes on the clinic yard.

Something is happening . . . must be an accident someplace. She watched as Josie ran to the clinic, stopped to talk to Beulah on the sidewalk, and then disappeared inside the building. Within minutes the women ran to the wagon, and she saw the horses pull the wagon away from the fence at a fast clip.

That looks like Jack Frey and his team and wagon. He was supposed to stop by for a visit but not for another hour when school is out for the weekend. Hhmm . . . . Thinking about the cowboy made her smile. Through the winter months he had come "a courtin' her and she enjoyed the attention. *He's a good looking cowboy if ever I saw one,* she thought. *I'll just catch him in the yard when he drives by . . . what? Where is he going?*

Sarah Marie stopped walking and watched the wagon box until it was out of her sight. She dropped her arm that had been frantically waving for Jack to stop. *Now I'll have to wait until they get back to find out what is going on in town.*

The children, restless for the day to be over, spilled out onto the wet lawn. Sarah Marie, now fully alert to her students, acted like a pretend "mother hen" swooshing her "little chicks" back through the open white door. Back inside, discipline took control and normalcy settled over them. Sarah picked up her book. *Guess I'll find out soon enough, but now I need to finish up this reading lesson.*

"I'm here, Milka! What's the matter? Are you all right? Frankie, Josie? Where are all of you?" Mr. Mutchnik used his pet name, Milka, for his wife, Mary. He was born in the "Old Country" and whenever he became excited, worried or pleased about something immediately taking place, he reverted to his original language.

Mr. Mutchnik pulled off his hat and hung it on the hall coat tree and kicked off his hard soled shoes, wet from crossing in the tall grass between the two buildings. He took a step into the living space and saw Dr. Martin lying prone on the bed with one of Mary's quilts tossed over her.

After his eyes adjusted to the darkened room, he spotted his Milka sitting in her wheelchair, holding Frankie on her lap, reading to him. The boy was almost asleep from the low tone of Mary's voice as she read, slowly, deliberately. Mary raised her finger to her lips and motioned to Mr. Mutchnik to be very quiet and to meet her in the kitchen. He waited until Mary had wheeled herself and the boy through the open doorway.

"What's happening Milka? I heard the bell and came as quickly as I could. Why is Doctor . . . ?" He stopped talking so he could take Frankie from Mary and jiggle him for a bit, doing a little dance with the boy. Frankie squealed with each step.

"We have unexpected company, dear." Mary nodded towards the other room. "It seems Dr. Martin's baby is about to join us this evening. She is resting now, waiting for Beulah and Josie to return any minute." Mary sighed. "We need a plan for Frankie and you." She wheeled herself over closer to Mr. Mutchnik. "Do you suppose you and Frankie could sleep in the mercantile tonight? There is a fold away couch in the back room that you could make do for one night, and Frankie already has a mattress in his play area." Mary looked around the kitchen. "We will eat as usual and Frankie can stay here with us women for a while, until we need for him to be away from the house."

Frankie, now playing on the round rag rug in the middle of the parlor was engrossed in stacking wooden blocks. He'd get them just so high and then knock over the precarious squares, giggling and clapping his hands.

"Why, this is surely unexpected, Milka. Shouldn't she be in the clinic?" Mr. Mutchnik pointed towards Dr. Martin who was not moving under the quilt.

"I suppose she should, but there isn't time and the weather is so frightful that it would be difficult to move her. Josie has gone to fetch Beulah."

"Then I'll wait with you until the women folk return." Mr. Mutchnik reached for a cup and poured himself a drink of the freshly boiled brew. He walked to the only soft chair in the house and sat down. "Do you remember helping Josie when she gave birth to Frankie?" He looked at the healthy young boy playing at his feet and smiled.

"Our lives certainly have taken a sharp turn on that pathway of adventure, wouldn't you say? Ever since Josie came into our boarding house in St. Louis things have been in high gear." He looked at his wife. "I am so sorry. Milka, that you are so broken."

"No time for that kind of talk. What is . . . is. I'm getting stronger every day, you can see that, and by summer time I'll be back inside the mercantile helping you with the books and doing many chores, even if it is while sitting in this contraption." She rubbed the tops of her legs. "Why, I call this chair my blessing, you old fool. At least I can get around." She paused for only a second.

"By the way, now isn't the best time to bring it up, but I will be needing a ramp built off the kitchen door so I can get outside these four walls come summer time."

"I'll have one of the workers build you the sturdiest ramp in town." They both laughed, causing Amelia to stir.

"Mary? Are you there? Josie isn't back with Beulah yet?"

Mary wheeled herself over to the bedside.

"Can I get you anything while you wait? Are you comfortable and warm?"

Amelia reached for Mary's hand. "I would like a drink of water, if you please?"

"Mr. Mutchnik could you bring us a glass of water, please?"

Mr. Mutchnik went to the water bucket and dipped out water into a canning jar.

Mary spoke low to Amelia. "You just be still for a while longer. Beulah and Josie are out in the rain, but will be here shortly. In fact, I think I hear something outside now."

~3~

Beulah

The horses started back down Broadway Avenue and the cowboy, known about town as Jack Frey, stomped a heavy boot onto the wagon brake, trying to slow the wagon's weight from pushing the horses. The mud was a problem and he found himself caught in a rut about 4 inches deep. The wagon stayed in the track, thankfully, and the horses completed the path to the bottom of the hill. Jack tipped back his cowboy hat and released the brake to full open.

Going down Main Street on Last Chance Gulch would present its own problems as other wagons were coming and going, bringing supplies from Ft. Benton to the mercantile stores. A wagon train had arrived early that morning, and bewildered travelers were still walking towards the various tents and shacks that greeted them. Even with the drizzling rain, people were scurrying to and fro, asking about hotels, cafés, wagons to rent and houses for sale. Many stayed inside their wagon, appreciating the canvas cover that served as a weather shield. Nothing in the way of shelter or a public cafe was in place yet. Helena was a tent town, made up of miners and drifters. Some families were braving it to come west.

"Helena grows with every new train, seems to me." Jack looked over at Josie. "I think that is the Overland Fiske outfit. Sarah Marie will be getting more children for her school."

Josie paid no attention to his banter but kept her eyes straight on the road. "If I have to jump off this wagon and run ahead of you, I will. Can't you go any faster?"

Beulah chuckled as she listened to Josie. "We have plenty of time, Miss Josie. We want to get there in one piece, right Mr. Jack?" Beulah hung on to the wagon box and she had a blanket tossed over her head to keep off the still falling rain. "First babies take a long time, Miss Josie. You remember your birthin' Frankie last year."

She wanted to pat the young woman on the back but the movement from the wagon kept her hanging on to her own seat. Beulah clamped her lips tight and huddled in the wagon box.

Seeing the Fiske wagon train parked on the main street, people teaming about, gave Beulah a start. *Mr. Fiske bein' home might not be a good thing for Dr. Amelia, Sarah Marie and me. We been boardin' at the Fiske house since last fall. Me doin' the cookin' and cleanin' might set okay with Mr. Fiske, but one just never knows about who can stay and go in a white man's house.*

Beulah tried to get her mind back to the problem at hand. *First off, we got to tend to Miss Amelia. My, my. It seems a lifetime ago I was dressing her for school. Here we are clear across the continent and living in a boarding house. Amelia has been through so much in such a short time. She graduated from medical school, married a fine young doctor, he gets himself killed. Now Miss Amelia herself a widow, moved out here and she is carryin' a baby. This is a far cry from what we dreamed about, but maybe the young'un will bring her some peace finally.* Beulah shut her eyes tight and shook the rain from her head.

Beulah was more than a domestic employee of Dr. Amelia Martin. Her ancestral family had been owned by Amelia's family back in the 1800s and had the distinction of being passed from father to son in the older gentleman's will. Young Beulah and her brother, Rufus had never worked anywhere else but for the Roberts' family. Rufus had the reputation of being the best blacksmith in the county and Beulah had been assigned to the house where she took care of the women's needs. When Amelia left for medical school, Beulah went with her. Now they were together in the god-forsaken, "Wild West".

After the Civil War, Amelia, Sarah Marie and Beulah sought adventure in the West. Beulah had acquired her freedman papers and was now a paid employee of Mrs. Elizabeth Fiske. She also worked as a paid employee in the medical clinic.

"Whoa!" shouted the driver. The team slid to a sudden stop in front of the Mutchnik house. The darkening evening sky, heavy with fog, made the day seem later than it really was. A lantern had been lit and set on the front porch steps. Josie jumped to the ground, remembered Beulah and reached for her hand to help her out of the wagon box. Jack grabbed the medical bag and hurried to the front door. It swung open on his first knock. He stepped back so the two ladies could enter.

"Well, it's about time you got here." Mr. Mutchnik smiled at the two women. Then he noticed the cowboy, hat in hand, still outside on the rickety porch.

"Hello Jack. Good to see you. How'd you get shanghaied into bringing back the two ladies to my house?"

Jack stepped into the warmth and light of the Mutchnik house. He sniffed boiling coffee and his nose wiggled a bit. *Now that's what we all need, is a good cup of Joe.*

"Howdy, Mr. Mutchnik."

Jack allowed his eyes to wander about the room until he saw Mary in the wheelchair. "Evening Ma'am . . . seems there's some excitement going on here tonight." He moved closer to her chair. "How's this chair working for you?" Jack bent down to look at the construction and how the four wheels were attached. A regular wood chair design had been followed, except the back legs had been cut shorter. A rod, with two small wooden wheels, probably taken from a child's toy, ran the length of the space between the chair legs, allowing the wheels to turn freely, but they did not swivel.

Mrs. Mutchnik spent most of her time going backwards as she pushed the chair around the room with her legs. She was able to scoot forward, also, but it was rather cumbersome and tiring for her to do so. In her alone time Mary drew designs of how the front wheels needed to turn. The problem came in what to use that would allow them to swivel. She also wanted very large wheels in the back that she could grab on to and push herself forward with much more ease.

"Hello, Mr. Frey. It's nice to see you again. Once again your wagon came to our rescue. I never did properly thank you for hauling me out of that rubble last fall and taking me to the clinic for medical help." Mary smiled at the tall, handsome cowboy.

"Glad to help, Ma'am. That explosion will be talked about for years to come." The cowboy shook his head and slowly stood up. The man and woman smiled at each other.

"Coffee is ready. Would you like a cup?" Mary scooted herself into the kitchen, motioning for Jack to follow her. "You'll have to serve yourself, if you don't mind. The extra cups are a bit higher than I can reach." She pointed to a plate of cookies on the counter. "Help yourself to the cookies. Made them fresh myself this morning."

Jack needed the black coffee and enjoyed two cookies before returning to the small living room where the women were seated. Miss Amelia lay very still on the bed in the other room, but Jack could tell the women were in tune with each other. The slightest movement from Amelia had Beulah hurrying to the bed.

"Ladies, do you need to move Dr. Martin to the clinic tonight?" Jack felt uneasy but was not going to leave if he could be of further help.

Mr. Mutchnik looked over at his wife. "Mary? What do you and the ladies think? I can take care of Frankie in the mercantile tonight, and you ladies can make do right here. I don't see any reason to take our guest out into that wet night, do you?"

Mary looked at Beulah. "I think she is best off right here, don't you, Beulah?" Mr. Frey can visit with Mr. Mutchnik in the mercantile and be on hand should we need anything from the clinic, wouldn't you agree?"

Beulah smiled. "I like that idea best of all, Miss Mary. Amelia will be so grateful to you for givin' up your bed for her. This might be a very long night, and she is best off with her friends helping her through this, bein' it's her firstborn."

She looked at Amelia and gave a start. "Oh! We need to get Sarah Marie here, too. She will never forgive us if we leave her out of her seeing her niece or nephew come into this world."

Jack jumped up from the wood chair he had been sitting on. "I'll go fetch her right now." He reached for his cowboy hat that someone had put on the hall tree, grabbed the blanket that Beulah had wrapped herself in earlier in the day, and headed for the door. "I'll bring Sarah Marie back, just tell Dr. Martin to wait a few minutes, hey?"

They all laughed at how nervous Jack seemed. "You might want to tend to that team of yours, too, young man," yelled Mr. Mutchnik out the open front door to the back of the departing cowboy.

"Yes sir. I'll see that they are fed and dry before too long."

"Be sure you come back here for supper, as the women will be getting busy making up something hot and you don't want to miss out on that." With that Mr. Mutchnik slammed the front door. "He'll be back. I saw him looking at that berry pie on the windowsill in the kitchen."

Jack Frey

~4~

Jack Frey

As the cowboy pulled his team away from the Mutchnik yard, he shivered. The fog hung low, moisture steamed into the air and the horses kept their heads closer to the ground than normal. They plodded along, no hurry this time to find the clinic, except Jack wanted to see Sarah Marie and bring her back to the activities at the Mutchnik house.

She'd never forgive any of us if we didn't include her tonight in this child-birthing of her sister. Jack shook his head and water swished off the hat brim, dripping onto his shoulders. His wool coat worked year 'round at keeping him warm, but tonight was unusually awful weather to be out riding in a wagon with no top.

How did I get right in the middle of this? Sure seems more than a coincidence I happened right then to be in Josie's path. He shrugged. *Hey! It gives me a chance to see Sarah Marie.* He clicked the horses to a little faster pace.

Through the fog Jack saw lanterns on porches. The glow seemed eerie in the swirls of fog, but he was glad to have the guidance as he worked his way up the dark street. The horses sensed they were headed back up Broadway Avenue and they turned automatically when they approached the bottom of the hill. Jack had not seen another wagon since he left the Mutchnik house.

Sure is quiet out here tonight. Not the best time for a birthing but I guess we don't have a choice when that hour comes. He was happy to call on Sarah Marie with the news. Any time he spent with her was always interesting.

Jack stopped the team at the Fiske white picket fence. He went through the gate and up the walk where he twisted the bell in the middle of the front door.

"Who are you?" asked an angelic voice from the other side of the door. "I can't open the door unless I know you. Do I know you?"

"I've come for Sarah Marie. Go get her for me please." Jack waited for what seemed forever, standing there in the rain. *They need a porch built on to the front of this house.* Just then the door opened and he saw a smiling Sarah Marie facing him.

"Why good evening, Mr. Frey. I have been waiting for you to call since this afternoon." She stepped aside and motioned for Jack to enter. "I saw you earlier at the clinic. You were certainly in a hurry." She took his hat and hung it on the hat rack pegs beside the door.

"I am sorry to be so late, Sarah Marie, but I am here to fetch you. Your sister is at the Mutchnik house and will not be coming home this evening." He smiled. "You are going to become an auntie tonight it sure does look like to me."

Sarah Marie reached for her cameo pinned at her throat. "Oh, my!" She stared at Jack. "What to do? I am feeding the children their supper since Beulah wasn't here to cook." She turned and started walking towards the kitchen. "Come with me, Jack and I'll give you a cup of coffee while I figure out what to do."

Sarah Marie and the children were cozy and warm in the bright yellow kitchen. They gave Jack a wave but continued to eat the stew in bowls set in front of them.

Jack noticed the six little ones were various sizes and ages. "Isn't Mrs. Fiske home? I thought I saw Mr. Fiske earlier with the Overland Wagon Train on the gulch."

Sarah Marie's face clouded and she looked frustrated. "You are correct, Jack. Mr. Fiske is indeed home. He and Mrs. Fiske have taken their dinner upstairs to his office where they can talk uninterrupted." She shrugged. "I guess I will just have to be the one to interrupt them, won't I?" With that Sarah Marie giggled.

"I do think Mrs. Fiske would prefer the baby be born at the Mutchnik house rather than here tonight." She looked around the room for a second pondering what to do.

"I am sure there is plenty of time, Jack. First babies take a while to decide they want to enter into this big scary place called "the world."" Jack was happy to see her staying in control and he smiled at her.

"I'm not going any place. The Mutchniks are making arrangements for Mr. Mutchnik and Frankie to stay in the mercantile building tonight. They were fixin' to make a hot supper when I left to come here." He sat down in the extra wood chair next to one of the children. "Umm. That stew looks mighty good." He pretended to grab a piece of meat out of the nearest bowl, and a howl came from the child. Jack pulled his hand back and laughed.

"Okay. Here's the plan. After the children finish, I'll clean up the kitchen. Then we can leave." Sarah Marie glanced up the stairway. "I'll be right back."

Jack watched her as she confidently climbed the flight of stairs and he heard her knock on a door on the second floor. *I wonder how this news is going to be accepted. Beulah and Sarah Marie both gone. She's going to have to do some tending to her own brood.* He fidgeted.

Sarah Marie would move out tonight in this awful rain if she gets a bad word from Mrs. Fiske. I sure don't want that to happen. Nothing will keep her from her sister's side tonight.

He heard Sarah Marie returning to the kitchen and he stood up. The children were finished and waited to be excused. "Children, I have an errand to run this evening and I won't be back until sometime tomorrow." She raised her hand like a stop sign. "Now promise me you will be good and obey your mother and father." She looked at each child, waiting for a "Yes, Ma'am" from each little body.

"Jack, I must clear the table, but I'll be ready to leave here in fifteen minutes."

"That's okay with me. My team needs to be fed and put into the stable, but I'll do that after I take you back to the Mutchnik house." *I'm also going to take time to have some supper and pie, too.*

Jack had not planned to spend the entire day and overnight in town. He had come in for ranch supplies when Josie intercepted him and before the rain began, bringing the spring storm. The idea of sleeping in the stable with his horses wasn't the best he'd had all day, but that's the way it was working out for him. At least he'd be out of the storm, and he'd be warm rolled into the hay. *I can always walk over to the mercantile building and sleep inside with Mr. Mutchnik and Frankie. That is what one of the women thought I should do.* Jack chuckled at that idea. *Women always seem to have a plan.*

Sarah Marie walked through the front door and noticed a light on in the clinic.

She turned to Jack. "We must make a quick stop at the clinic, too. Dr. Rodney is probably wondering where everyone is tonight." She smiled at him. "He is going to have to be available for any emergencies through the night." Sarah Marie tossed a blanket over her head and ran quickly toward the wagon where the horses patiently waited for their master. "Do horses feel all that water on their backs?"

Jack thought a minute. "Naw! Their hide is so thick they don't feel it." Just then one of the animals snickered a welcome, and then shook his whole giant body. Water splashed in all directions, soaking Jack's wool coat.

~5~

Sarah Marie

Jack hurried Sarah Marie down the dark path to the saturated wagon box. He flipped off the rain from the bench seat, spread the blanket for Sarah Marie to sit on, and helped his lady friend into the wagon. Her skirts were catching on the splinters on the side of the box. She had brought a heavy, hooded cloak along with a blanket to wrap around her legs to keep them from getting soaked.

"Sorry about the wet seat, Sarah Marie, but I can't do much about the weather." Jack grimaced as she sat down on the damp blanket. "I'll make it a quick trip for you."

Sarah Marie grabbed on to the wagon seat bar to steady her body as the wagon jostled about in the muddy ruts. She drew her lips into a tight line and concentrated on the road. The smell from the wet horses was not something she was used to, and she wished she had a handkerchief to spread across her nose and mouth.

Leave it to you, Amelia, to be away from the clinic on a night like this and your baby deciding it's time to be born. I'm glad you are with the Mutchniks. Beulah can tend to you and Josie care for the household. I am praying for you, dear sister. Wait for me to get there. I'm coming. Mr. Frey is doing the best he can on this dark night.

Sarah Marie prayed in silence, the only noise an occasional snicker from the horses. She watched as steam rolled off the animals' backs.

I'll not forget this night. I can't believe how penetrating that fog is. She jumped when a dog barked near the right front wagon wheel. The horses shied to the left as Jack shouted out to the team to behave themselves.

Kind of reminds me of our home in Virginia. Nights like this one really make me long to see Mother and Father again. Sarah Marie sighed. *How excited they will be to know they are grandparents to their first grandchild. Amelia told me not to write them her news about being with child, but now I can. Tomorrow will be letter writing day. I've grown and matured so much since last October. I feel like a very old maid aunt right now.* She looked over to view Jack's solid face.

Now, Jack just fits the bill for my meeting a rich cowboy. Sarah Marie smiled and even chuckled out loud as she thought about her criteria that her cowboy would have to be rich. *I wonder if he's rich? Probably not yet, but he's going to own land and be somebody very soon. He told me on his last visit that he planned to get some homesteading land in the next government grab. Maybe he'll think about taking me for his bride.* Sarah sat up straighter on the bench, trying to not disclose how uncomfortable she was. Virginia seemed a far ways away as Sarah Marie sat, cold and shivering on the hard bench of a lumbering farm wagon.

Staring into the darkness, Sarah Marie decided she wanted to talk. She could use this time to get to know Jack Frey better, too. *I wonder if he'll tell me anything about where he is from and what he used to do. What kind of a childhood did he have?*

The cowboy concentrated on the team and the muddy road.

"Women are like teabags;

you

never know how strong

they are

until they're put in hot water."

- Eleanor Roosevelt -

Josie

~6~

Frank's Letter to Josie

The rain finally stopped pelting the weathered boards of the houses and Frankie had fallen asleep in his little bed inside the Mutchnik house. Amelia knew her time was getting closer as the contractions were closer together. She was not uncomfortable yet but some restlessness had worked its way into her body and spirit.

Beulah had everything under control, and Josie decided she would use this break to take Frankie across to the mercantile and get both Mr. Mutchnik and Frankie settled in for the night. She scooped up her son who was sound asleep in front of the fireplace. She hoped the cool night air would not rouse him too much.

"Mr. Mutchnik." Josie softly called his name. "I am sorry to wake you from your nap on the couch, but I do think we need to take Frankie to his mattress." She motioned to the dimly lit kerosene lamp casting shadows on the walls in the parlor. "Be sure and bring the lamp, please."

Mr. Mutchnik woke with a start. "Is she about to give birth?"

"Not yet and I am not sure that it is even near. I just want to get Frankie into a warm sleeping area and not miss being here. I plan to stay with you two for a while in case he wakes up and misses me. I don't want you to have to come back to the house with him later tonight." Josie sighed. "This might be a long night for all of us."

The older man traded Josie the lamp for the boy. "Here. You take the lamp, and let me carry Frankie now that I have my shoes on. Wrap him tight and cover his head, too. We don't want him catching a spring chill."

Josie smiled as she reached for the stack of blankets and a pillow. She held the lamp in her left hand and used her backside to push open the kitchen door that luckily was not latched.

Jack Frey had left some hours ago, saying he would spend the night at the stable which was only a street away from the mercantile building. "Just send for me if you need me in a hurry. Otherwise, I'll be up and around early in the morning. Not much left of tonight."

He disappeared into the black night. Josie heard him shout out, "Tell Sarah Marie I'll be by for breakfast." The clanking of the wagon wheels drowned out any other conversation as the animals, also in need of shelter and food, were anxious to be where it was dry.

When Josie walked into the mercantile office it surprised her to see the books still open on the desk top, the doors unlocked, and a stack of greenbacks tucked into the corner of the felt blotter pad on the desk. A hastily scrawled note said, *"We didn't see you leave. We bought a shovel and here is the money."* It was signed by a name Josie did not recognize, *Robert Payne.*

So many newcomers every day coming in to Helena. At least these people were honest. She gave a tired sigh. *I'll try to remember this name and thank them for their business.*

She sat down at the desk and noticed a stack of letters. Among her many duties, Josie served as the postmistress for the community. She had set up small boxes alphabetically against one inside wall for people to claim and check their mail.

Sometimes, if a letter sat for too long and Josie knew the person, she would go for a walk, hand delivering the mail. Many letters went unclaimed if the party could not be found. Josie had a special box for these letters, hoping they would be claimed some day. She never wanted to send the letters back and held on to them for months.

Postage was high, and most letters did not have a return address visible on the envelope. There was no special rule or law about what to do with the unclaimed letters. Occasionally, a man would wander in to town from the mines and check the letter names. If he recognized the name, he'd pocket the letter. Josie had heard of letters being out in the "field" for months before the proper person was found. "Dead" letters were opened by Josie and if a name and address was inside the envelope on the letter itself, she would return the letter to the sender, paying the postage from her own purse. She felt it was the right thing to do for the families. The movement west brought all types of people through the territories. Families would stop, hoping to begin a new life in a new community. The groups that stayed became the backbone of Helena.

Well, I guess I'll go through this stack first thing. Frankie didn't even whimper when I put him into the corner play pen area and he is warm and secure on his blanket mattress. Sarah Marie and Beulah and Mary can handle the birthing. I'll kind of wander between the two buildings. If Beulah needs me, she'll holler.

She looked over at her baby son. Her eyes filled with tears from the love she had for the little fellow who depended upon her for his very life. *Jeremiah, how I miss you. Please watch over me and your son and help him grow into the kind of man you were.* Josie turned away from the boy and started sorting the United States Postal mail.

Well, I'll be. This letter is addressed to Mrs. Jeremiah Hicks, Helena, Montana Territory. She examined the envelope and noticed the Virginia post mark inked over the stamp. She raised her eyebrows in a frown. *No one calls me Mrs. Hicks. I still am known as Mrs. Hill. That will have to be corrected very soon. It is a good thing that the Mutchnik's know my true name. They have kept my secret that no longer needs to be kept. Dr. Martin calls me Mrs. Josie Hill, as do other townspeople.*

It's from Frank Hicks. My, my. I wonder why he is writing me? Josie carefully opened the envelope and pulled out a single piece of lined white writing paper, the kind one tears out of a child's Indian Head school pad.

Josie looked for Mr. Mutchnik but he was in the back uncovering that couch he knew was in the back area of the building. He planned to drag it front and center so he would be near Frankie should the boy wake up in the night. He also planned to leave the lamp at a low glow to ward off the darkness should little Frankie wake up and be confused by his surroundings.

In silence Josie read her letter from Frank Hicks, dated February 10, 1876.

Dear Josie,

I am sorry I did not write you after Jeremiah's accident and death.

I read Jeremiah's letter to me over and over. I am happy you named your little boy after me. He must be a fine little lad by now?

My news is this. I sold the farm here in Virginia to Dr. Roberts, who is Dr. Amelia Martin's father. Is Amelia practicing medicine in Helena as visioned?

I will be arriving in Ft. Benton late Fall of this year. I plan to come up river to join the Hicks' family. I have applied for land near Helena in an area called Wolf Creek. Hopefully, we will become acquainted before the year is out.

Sincerely,
Frank Hicks

Josie's hand began trembling and she didn't know why. It would be nice to have Frank Hicks nearby and be an uncle to her boy. *Why am I shaking?* Josie picked up the letter and reread its message. Slowly she thought about Dr. Martin being from Virginia.

No. She can't be the lost girlfriend that Jeremiah told her about when they were camped by the river. Can she be? Josie was puzzled by her thoughts. *No. That can't be. Amelia would have said something by now if it were true.*

But again a dark thought passed through her mind. *Maybe that is her secret past? Oh, my goodness! That would explain her devotion to my little Frankie. He looks just like his father. She would see Jeremiah every time she looks at my boy.*

Josie jumped up and started to pace the room. Just then Mr. Mutchnik came in huffing and puffing from pulling the heavy ornate couch out of the back storage area.

Josie went to help him and, without a word to him, she made up a bed out of the blankets and pillow she had brought with her from the house a few hours earlier. The tension lay between them so heavy that Mr. Mutchnik made comment.

"Josie? What is wrong, my dear? Something has happened. Did you get some word from the house?"

"No, no, nothing like that. I am just very tired from this very long, very dreary day." She turned from him, not wanting him to see the trickle of tears pushing at the corners of her eyes.

~7~

Joseph James Martin

With great effort, Josie forced herself back inside the dimly lit Mutchnik house.

How am I going to be able to face Amelia? She needs all the support we women can give her during this time. Josie stood at the kitchen table, and gave a short wave to Mary Mutchnik. Mary joined her in the kitchen and put her index finger to her mouth. "Just whisper. Amelia is sleeping at the moment."

Beulah felt the fresh air that blew inside the house when Josie opened the door. She had been dozing in the only soft cushioned chair, but was now fully awake. She checked on Amelia, put her hand on Amelia's forehead and frowned.

"Amelia. Amelia . . . wake up, Missy. I want to help you get up out of this bed. You need to take a walk around the room for a bit and get things moving." Beulah gently pulled back the covers. "Come on, now. Let's help this baby."

Beulah started humming a favorite hymn that she sang when she midwifed at the clinic. How many babies had she delivered over the past year? More than she cared to count. Experience had taught Beulah and Dr. Martin that each baby comes at its own speed and time.

Amelia, fully awake, slipped her feet over the edge of the bed, but could go no further. She raised her hands up to Beulah. "Help me, Beulah. For some reason this baby is not willing to move down the birth canal and out of me." Amelia bit her lip. "This is taking way too long. I feel strong yet, but it is two o'clock in the morning, and we need to change the plans." Amelia thought a minute. "Did you bring any herbs and teas with you?"

Beulah nodded that she had. She turned to Josie. "Would you please make sure we have hot water on the wood stove? I think we will be needin' it very soon." Beulah turned back to Amelia. "One cup of herbal tea will be at the kitchen table waitin' for you to walk over to get it."

Beulah smiled as she helped Amelia to her feet. "Let's get this baby into swaddlin' clothes right soon now."

A very concerned and tired Sarah Marie located the gauze packet of ground up herbs and poured a teaspoonful into a mug of hot water. To sweeten the bitter taste she added honey. "Will this help induce labor?"

Beulah and Amelia both nodded at the same time. Beulah answered Sarah Marie's question. "We use this in first birth females if there seems to be a problem getting contractions closer together. The herb relaxes some tension buildup so that the muscles can do the necessary pushing to get baby front and center." Amelia walked to the table and put both hands on the oilcloth cover. She visibly showed signs of fatigue but she did not verbalize her fear that something might be wrong.

"Here, sister. Sit down before you fall down." Sarah Marie shoved a wood kitchen chair behind Amelia. Just as quickly, Beulah removed it.

"No, Missy. She needs to walk a bit." Beulah motioned to Sarah Marie to take one arm while she latched on to her right one. "Let's make a turn around the house, Amelia. We have you supported and you are doing just fine." Beulah smiled, but her eyes squinted and she had a wary face. Around and around they walked until Amelia finally moved toward the bed.

"It's time. My baby is coming this very morning." Amelia smiled as Beulah helped her lie back on the pillows and get into the birthing position. She put a canvas bag filled with sand beneath each foot to hold her legs in a bent angle. This would help Amelia to push and bear down to help the baby make an entrance.

Josie was frozen in time. She had not moved from the kitchen door area and she had not spoken to any of them. Without thinking, she turned on her heel and retreated outside. She had to catch her breath. Her mind would not let her erase what she thought she knew about Amelia and Jeremiah.

This is just more than I need to face right now. Why did she not tell me?

We will have to talk about this some day very soon. I must know the true story. I believe Jeremiah loved me. He was so happy with little Frankie when he saw him for the first time at the river's edge in Ft. Benton. We had such a grand reunion that day.

Josie put one hand on her waist and the other on her forehead. *I was the woman he married. Did he know she was here in Helena and that is why he wanted to come here?* She squeezed back tears. *No, I know better than that. He wouldn't have married me in St. Louis if that were true. He is the one who did not want to keep lying about us.*

Josie did not know how long she stood outside on the Mutchnik porch, but she was chilled to the bone when she decided to return to the house and do whatever she could to help Amelia through her ordeal.

I'll continue to be her friend. We have so much in common now, both widows with a young child. Our children will play together; go to school and church together. And what is just is. Maybe I won't even tell her what I know. I'll have to think about it. Would it do any good? We both loved the same person, but she loved the boy. I loved the man and the father of my little Frankie.

A scream pierced the air. Josie jumped at the sound but it was enough to get her back inside. Beulah and Sarah Marie were busy helping Amelia. Beulah was reaching for the crowning head. Sarah Marie was wiping her brow. Both were coaching.

"Push Amelia. One more time." Amelia pushed. "Good girl. We are on our way now." Beulah worked quickly and with a smooth move, pulled the baby from Amelia and shouted "Halleluiah" into the room. Mrs. Mutchnik, who had deliberately stayed out of the way, rolled into the bedroom. She had a family Bible in her lap.

"What'd we get? A boy or a girl? I've got to record the birth time, place and name."

Amelia looked at the women surrounding her bed. She held her new baby on her stomach and stroked the little body so tenderly. Her eyes were glistening with tender love for this tiny baby, forever uniting her to her husband, Dr. James Martin, Deceased.

"Our baby is a boy and his name is Joseph James Martin. Today is March 19th and it is the feast day of St. Joseph." A tear slid down her cheek. "Welcome, little Joseph. I've been waiting for you for a very long time."

Beulah finished her midwifery duties and wrapped the newborn in swaddling clothes. She handed Joseph back to his mother, cradling pillows around her left arm.

"You did just right, Missy. Now, how about you takin' a little nap? We'll be right here to care for your young'un."

A collective sigh rose into the early morning air. Mary made the necessary marks in her Bible, and then wheeled herself into the kitchen. "We need coffee."

~8~

The Next Morning

Beulah, though fatigued by the long hours of the day and the midwifery that lasted through the evening and into the wee hours of the morning, couldn't help feeling alive and happy. She was a bit smug as she thought about her part in helping Miss Amelia through her delivery of Joseph James Martin.

I've come such a long ways with Miss Amelia. We are more like family than even she suspects. I would reckon so. Beulah looked over at the sleeping mother and child. *The future is nothin' but brightness and happiness for them now.*

The baby stirred. Amelia instantly opened her eyes and looked at her bundle of joy. Beulah walked to the bed and took the infant from Amelia for a few minutes, while humming an old Negro spiritual so softly only the baby could hear. He looked towards the noise and Beulah was sure she saw him smile at her. *He smiles behind his eyes. That's just like his daddy did, too. What a shame, a real shame that Dr. Martin couldn't live to see his own son being born.* She shook her head. *Here he's born in an old shack instead of the fancy mansion in Virginia. That was another world for all of us, and certainly for this here young'un.* She returned the infant to his mother's waiting arms.

Beulah and Sarah Marie had tidied up the room before taking leave of the Mutchnik house. They needed a much-deserved rest for what was left of the morning.

It was their intention to walk to the stable and have Mr. Frey hitch the wagon and give them a ride. Even though a stroll in the brisk spring air would have been enjoyable, they both were too exhausted to even consider the idea of walking back to the boarding house near the clinic.

"At least the rain has stopped." Sarah Marie turned her face upward to look for stars.

"Yes, Miss Sarah Marie. It will be a beautiful March day when that old sun decides to wake up slow and lazy like." Beulah carried her medical bag while Sarah Marie held on to the extra blankets they had covered themselves with earlier while riding in the open wagon in the rain.

"Will we leave Amelia with Mary for a few days?" I do believe Mrs. Fiske would prefer that since Mr. Fiske is now home and the children will be curious soon enough with a new baby in the house." Beulah nodded her head as she knocked on the wooden slat door of the stable barn. "Josie can tend to her while we rest up a bit."

A horse nickered, and the women heard movement on the other side of the door.

"I'm up. I'm up. Just a minute."

The door opened and there stood the handsome cowboy, hay sticks and all, with a curious smile. "Is the baby here? Everything okay?"

He stepped aside. "Ladies do come inside. That air is mighty brisk this morning." He looked up at the sky. "It is morning, isn't it?"

Sarah Marie knew she was in love. "Yes, to everything you ask, Mr. Frey." She smiled as she stepped further into the stable. "I am sorry about you not getting breakfast, but Beulah and I both need rest and we would like a ride back to the clinic if we can persuade you to give us one." She looked right into his eyes and she just knew . . . she was in love.

Jack Frey chuckled. "A ride, huh? Is that all I'm good for is hauling you ladies around Helena at all hours of the day and night and in all kinds of weather?" He reached for his boots. "You make yourselves comfortable on a couple of those old benches while I hitch up the team and I'll have you home in record time." He looked at the cold stove, but didn't whine for a cup of coffee to get him started for the day.

Sarah Marie waited until he had gone into the back side of the barn to bring around his team of horses to harness them and then hitch them to the wagon.

"I can make a fire and there is a coffee pot on top of that pot-bellied stove." She opened the door and tossed in some kindling she found alongside the stove

"There's a bit of water in that drinking bucket. I'll make him some coffee if there is anything in that pot from yesterday." She stuck her nose into the pot. "Oh. It's awful. But whatever those grounds are will have to do."

Within a few minutes she had a warm fire going and a pot of water boiling. She even found a dented tin cup that she filled with the hot liquid just as her cowboy came back.

"Well, would you look at this? I smelled your coffee clear back there." He pointed to the rear of the building. "It will taste like nectar of the gods. Thank you." He took a long gulp and tossed the empty cup on top of a shelf.

Sarah Marie knew he was being kind, but he seemed to appreciate her efforts.

"Let's be on our way, then. I hope to get some rest before we have to start the day. Thank God it is Saturday and the children will not be waiting for school."

Beulah glanced over at the other two. "Sure 'nough okay for you but me? Why, I have to get breakfast for that brood and since Mr. Fiske is here, he's going to want a fancy spread, mark my word." Beulah sighed.

"It was worth every bit of the lost sleep being there tonight, wasn't it, Miss Sarah Marie? Your sister, why she did a fine job of birthin' her precious boy child."

The women waited by the front door when they heard the rattle of harness.

"Your chariot awaits. Step carefully, now, ladies." Mr. Frey helped each woman into the wagon, seeing to it that Sarah Marie sat next to him on the board. As before, he spread a blanket on the seat first. He brought the long side of the blanket up over the legs of the two women, trying to keep the chill off of them. They found their way up Last Chance Gulch to the hill that would take them up Broadway Avenue and back to the Fiske boarding house on Rodney Street. He did not urge the horses but let them set their own pace.

"My goodness, but I had forgotten what a ways we were from the Mutchnik house. This is such a special treat. We do thank you for the ride." Sarah Marie paused as if in thought. "Thank you for all of the rides, coming and going these past hours." It was with perfect intent she smiled a dazzling smile that lit up her face, erasing the tired lines around her eyes. She outstretched her petite hand and just for a second rested it upon the cowboy's arm. Her hand felt warm and familiar and he did not pull away.

Mr. Frey swiftly unloaded his precious ladies and took immediate leave.

I am in need of a good cup of coffee. That stuff at the stable should be buried in the corral. It's not fit for human consumption. He made a grimace as if erasing a bad taste from his mouth, but instead a smile spread across his face and he decided to whistle a tune as the team's harness jangled in the morning stillness. He watched as lamp light appeared in windows along the route. Morning had come to Helena, Montana Territory, and what a great day it was going to be.

I'll go back to the stable. By now, Jake will be there to tend to the boarded horses. He'll have some sour dough pancake starter and we'll take care of my growling stomach.

~9~

Beulah

Two weeks later found the Mutchniks, Josie and Frankie, back together in their home. Amelia felt strong enough to return to the Fiske boarding house. The baby was a night sleeper and did not cause much of a disturbance for the Fiske family. They were used to the sounds of a newborn, especially after their twins had arrived a few years ago.

Sarah Marie, lost in her own thoughts and dreams, returned to her classroom that following Monday, wondering when her cowboy would once again be making a trip into Helena for supplies. She hoped every day that he would knock on her door, and every evening, when he had not done so, she'd said a prayer that he was in good health and thinking about her.

Only Beulah was restless. She wondered where the handyman was keeping himself. Usually Moses arrived on Monday to do chores for Mrs. Fiske. He brought wagon loads of wood from the Wolf Creek Mountains where he had a cabin up Rose Creek. He chopped wood, made kindling strips of wood, and kept the supply in a shed by the outhouse. He rigged a lock on the door. Wood was so scarce people would steal it during the night.

Mrs. Fiske always kept a generous supply of wood by the kitchen stove and it was Moses' job to keep that bin full of kindling sticks as well. The Fiske house was a large structure that relied on coal to keep it warm, but wood to cook by. Wood was burned in the fireplaces on both floors, in the study and sitting room.

A coal supplier freighted coal from the coal fields east of Helena every fall. The coal chute opened on the far side of the mansion, out of sight from the street. Beulah had never seen such a dusty mess as the day they delivered the coal. It was dry, dusty and in large chunks that the men broke up into shovel sized lumps. Dust flew everywhere in that basement dugout and came up through the staircase and the flues. For weeks afterward a daily cleaning was required of her to get rid of the black grit that landed everywhere.

Here it is March and I'm still washin' grit. Beulah had just hung several room rugs to air on the line strung near the kitchen door. She beat at them with a wire whisk, taking out her frustrations.

I can't understand where Moses is. Why, there is spring work for him to do all over town. Mr. Mutchnik said supplies were arriving any day now from Ft. Benton, and freight wagons can be seen for miles stretching across the Prickly Pear Valley. Beulah stopped for a minute to give her arm a rest.

Her eyes gazed out over the valley floor. Mountain tops circled the skyline in all directions. The town set down like the flat bottom of a mixing bowl. Snow mantled the ground above timberline. The view constantly changed with the seasons.

I think Moses likes me. I know I sure do want him to come courtin' me. He was the first black man I met when we got here; I think he was as happy to see me as I was to see him. Mrs. Fiske had him bring in our trunks and I was amazed at how strong he was; he just slung that trunk up onto his shoulder and walked clear into the house with it. He wasn't even strainin' his muscles. Beulah smiled. *So much has happened to me.* She shook her head back and forth as if trying to make sense of her thoughts.

Laws, where is that man? I have a list of chores for him to get started on and we can visit some, too. I wonder where he stays when he comes to town. She chuckled. *He treats that broken down old mule of his like it was a thoroughbred stallion meant for royalty.* Moses also had a pet dog, a black and white herder. He rode in the wagon with him most of the time. The dog slept in the shade of the wagon when Moses worked for white people. He did not play with children unless Moses gave him the command to "fetch the stick."

The mule, broke to pull a small wagon, had been with Moses ever since he left the Union Army after the Civil War. He was hired as a woodchopper to keep the cooks' fires burning. The supply clerk gave him his discharge papers, along with some beans and tobacco, a paycheck and a 50-70 Gov. Springfield rifle. It had a converted trap door and though beat up looking, Moses was more than happy to take the firearm. The clerk tossed in the mule and wagon as a bonus and Moses took everything offered him. He was happy to keep the mule and wagon for future use

He was headed west where a new life awaited him and the others who were travelling together. "Safety in numbers" was their password. Even though the war was officially over, most of the country did not know that news, and caution was the key to making it out of the south. Bands of robbers would attack a lone man.

Beulah did not see any sign of a mule or dust from wagon wheels in the distance. *Well, if he is in town he'll be comin' around. I made a pumpkin-squash pie from the fall harvest still keepin' in the storage shed. He'll not turn down a piece of that pie.* Beulah quickly entered the bright Fiske kitchen, leaving the rugs to flap in the breeze.

Thinkin' of Moses makes me think of my brother, Rufus. Some day I hope to see him again. I keep writin' him to make the move west. One day he will. I'll jess keep on prayin' for that happy day. He could open a blacksmith shop, a boardin' stable for animals, work on a ranch, why he'd fit in anywhere he wanted to. Beulah grabbed the water bucket off the counter and returned outside to the well. She needed fresh water.

It'll soon be time for lunch and the children will be hungry. She thought a minute. *What do I have left over in my pantry? I think a trip to the mercantile is in order. I'll get Robert to go with me and he can pull his little wagon. He'll like getting time out of school.* Sarah Marie would see to it that Beulah had a companion to pull the wagon.

Working for the Fiske family proved a good match for Beulah. She recognized how Mrs. Fiske needed to be in control of her household and Beulah accepted the occasional unpleasant encounters over something usually very trivial. Beulah and Sarah Marie were doing a wonderful job in guiding the Fiske children through their different levels of education, age and sibling problems. Mrs. Fiske was happy to leave the children in their care as she longed to be part of the elite society of Helena. She attended luncheons and teas and also hosted events in her home. She kept Beulah very busy with her clothes needing attention, and specialty cookies and tea sandwiches made fresh the day of the event.

The oldest Fiske daughter, Corrine, age thirteen, proved to be a big help to Amelia with the baby. She cared for the Fiske twins when they were born a few years ago. While the other children were curious about the new baby in the house, they didn't hover like Corrine.

After school hours and on weekends, Amelia hired Corrine whenever she needed someone to watch Joseph while she worked with a patient at the clinic, or took a rest break. During the day Amelia kept Joseph with her at the clinic. Everything was working out very nicely, except for one thing. The mystery grew daily as to where Moses was keeping himself these past two weeks.

Beulah had just put away the last of the dinner dishes and had swept up the kitchen floor when she heard shouts coming from the yard. Mr. Fiske, working in his study on the second floor of the house, came galloping down the bare wood stairs and flung open the front door. He was silhouetted in the lamp light that spilled out onto the grass.

"Who's there? What's all the shouting about?"

"Mr. Fiske!" shouted the man. "There you are. Have you heard about the murder?" He paused and waited for Mr. Fiske to say something. When he didn't, the rider continued, his voice anxious. "You know that black feller who does handyman work for your Missus?"

He raised his hand in greeting at the same time he slid off the saddle, landing both boots onto the ground. His horse, nervous and sweating with foam, danced a bit in a half circle while the rider tied the reins to the hitching post by the front gate.

"Yes. Of course I know the man. Get on with your story."

Beulah stood in the shadow of the house, shivering but not from the cold wind. Something was terribly wrong. She knew it all along when Moses hadn't been to town to see her. *What does this man know? Please, Lord, let it be that he is jess badly hurt, not dead, murdered.*

Mr. Fiske walked over to the messenger and grabbed him by the arm. "Out with it, man. Tell me what you know." He held on to the man's arm, not wanting him to bolt.

"Somebody shot that feller through his cabin window. Been dead a few days. Flies and stench gets you way before you open the cabin door." He looked at Mr. Fiske. "We gotta go tell the Sheriff, I reckon."

"Yes, we'll go find the Sheriff, but first you have to tell me what you know, saw, heard, anything connected with this crime." He led the man to the front door and brought him into the kitchen. Beulah had scurried inside just moments before, not wanting to be caught eavesdropping on their conversation out in the yard.

Mr. Fiske started barking orders to Beulah. "Beulah, get us some fresh coffee. I need pencil and paper from my study. Tell Mrs. Fiske to keep the children upstairs." "Yes, suh." Beulah put water in the coffeepot, set it on the back stove grate, grabbed for cups to place on the table, ran up the stairs to the study and fetched paper and pencil. She knocked on Mrs. Fiske's sitting room door and when she opened it, Beulah gave her the message. She ran back to the kitchen. The coffee was ready and she poured two cups for the men.

She dawdled in the pantry pretending to be looking for cookies, cream, or other things to set out for the men to eat with their coffee.

"I was out huntin' up Rose Creek when I came up real slow like on a secret cabin that I didn't know was there. It wasn't there last fall I can tell you that much." The stranger took a big gulp of coffee and grabbed for a cookie.

"Keep your mind on your story," shouted Mr. Fiske. "What did you see?" He sat with his pencil poised over the pad of paper wanting to write down the facts of this case for his newspaper headlines for tomorrow's edition. This was big news. It had been awhile since there had been trouble with the gold seekers who lived in the hills around Helena.

Hundreds of men had secret cabins, mere shacks for humans and their mules, dogs, and maybe a few chickens. Moses at least had eggs and sour dough starter to keep away the hunger pains when they hit. The lure of finding gold struck most every man who ventured west with the dream of finding the elephant. Most moved into town come winter but apparently Moses stayed weekends or longer at the cabin, coming into town to make day money.

The rider continued his story. "He was in the Kiyuse Saloon over on Wood Street a couple of weeks ago braggin' about findin' gold after he'd had a few rounds. The bartender showed us the gold nuggets that paid for the bottle of whiskey and shot glass. He even paid for the glass since the bartender intended to smash it after he left."

"Yeah, yeah!" Mr. Fiske waved his hand toward the man. "Get on with it." He shifted in his kitchen chair and stared right at the messenger.

"Okay. I'm a gettin' there. When I rode up real slow a mule brayed. So I got off my horse and walked up to the cabin door." He wrinkled his nose. "Like I said, it stunk all right." Mr. Fiske was growing impatient.

"I called out a 'Hello' but no one answered. That's when I saw him slumped on the floor." He paused. "He was dead, all right. I didn't have to touch him to know."

The man stood up and stretched his legs. "I skedaddled out of there as fast as my horse could travel and I came right here first. I figured you'd know what to do, bein' as you run the newspaper."

"You did right, fella. Fiske stared at the young man, with hard, steel-gray eyes. "You do it for the gold you thought he might have hidden out there? Tell me the truth." He smiled at the stranger. "Was there anything else worth taking?"

The rider cringed and shook his head violently. "No way. I ain't no murderer."

He grabbed the edge of the table top. "I'll take you and the Sheriff out there in the morning." It was a long, all day ride to the Wolf Creek Canyon. Most likely, the Sheriff and deputy would plan to stay overnight in the canyon gathering the body, evidence, papers, and things to identify who the dead man was. "I need to get some grub for me, put my horse in the stable and get him fed, too. I plan to sleep in the stable."

Beulah gasped. Mr. Fiske then remembered her lingering in the pantry area of the large kitchen. "Beulah, go tell Mrs. Fiske I am leaving the house to find the Sheriff."

The two men found Sheriff Seth Bullock sitting in his office reading by a kerosene lantern. When the men burst through the jailhouse door, he jumped up, startled.

"I didn't hear you two ride up. What brings you out this late?" He looked from one man to the other. "Grab a chair." He pointed to the two hard-backed chairs leaning against the windowless wall to the left of his desk.

"Sheriff, this young fella has a story to tell you. He came to me first not knowing where else to go since he is a stranger to this town."

The men shook hands. Then the sheriff turned to the stranger. "What's your name, son?"

"I'm not a face on one of those "Wanted" posters you was a lookin' at when we came in." He sat down alongside of Mr. Fiske. "I'm from the Dakota Territory out here looking for work. He paused a moment. "I go by Jacob Johanason. My Pa has a homestead."

The sheriff smiled. "I come from the Dakotas myself. Been a few years though." He walked around the desk to sit on the front edge. "Okay. Now that we have that out of the way, Jacob, tell me your story."

It took a while to tell the sheriff all that he knew about the dead man in the cabin, but the sheriff listened intently, not interrupting him.

"In the morning light you and I and a deputy will ride out there. You be back here by five o'clock ready to ride. Take your horse down the street to the stable that the Payne boys built. Tell them the sheriff will pay your board bill for your horse. They can put you up in the hotel since you need a place to sleep tonight. They serve early breakfasts so get some grub in the morning." He turned away, as if to dismiss the men, but he stopped the stranger.

"Tell them to make us up some travelling food for a couple of days for three men, too. We'll want water in canteens, and I want a dozen cans of tomatoes in the order." Mr. Fiske looked surprised. "Tomatoes?"

"We need moisture once we get into the canyon and to the dead man's place. Who knows what he has for a water supply."

The sheriff waved off the two men. Mr. Fiske did not ask to ride along. He knew he'd get the story first—hand when the men returned in a couple of days. His newspaper would have a story worthy of national attention. For the first time that evening, Mr. Fiske smiled.

Jacob parted company with the older men and rode his tired and hungry horse to the comfort and safety of the stable. *I'm so tired I can sleep in the hayloft. That is a long ways back across that valley into the Wolf Creek Canyon. The sheriff didn't say if he planned to take a team and wagon, but what else can he do to bring in the body? Hmmm. I guess he could strap him to the old guy's mule.* He yawned. *I'll tell him in the morning that there is a mule and a wagon already at the cabin.*

Just as Jacob was shutting his eyes, he sat straight up in the hay. *That sheriff back there. He said he was from the Dakotas. I remember we had a sheriff named Bullock who worked out of Deadwood and was there when Wild Bill Hickok got shot. He was the one who found the cards held in Wild Bill's hand, aces and eights, called the Dead man's hand. Bullock's one mighty tough hombre. He'll make Montana Territory safe for all of us pouring in to this valley. I'll be proud to ride with him in the morning.*

Jacob settled back down in the hay, crossed his hands on his chest, sighed a happy sigh and shut his eyes, hoping for sleep, knowing it would evade him. Dawn broke early and a stiff, groggy young man stretched himself. *Well, I might as well get my boots on and get to my duties. I need a thick-as-mud cup of coffee, that's all.*

(Thirty-four years after the crime was committed, the murder of Moses was solved. The guilty man, claiming self-defense, was arrested in Spokane, Washington. He was acquitted of the crime.)

Warshin' Clothes

Build fire in backyard to heat kettle of rain water.
Set tubs so smoke won't blow in eyes if wind is pert.
Shave one hole cake of lie soap in boilin' water.

Sort things, make 3 piles
1 pile whites
1 pile colored
1 pile work britches and rags.

To make starch, stir flour in cool water to smooth,
Then thin down with boilin' water.
Take white things, rub dirty spots on board, scrub hard,
And boil,
Then rub colored. Don't boil just wrench and starch.
Take things out of kettle with broom stick handle,
Then wrench, and starch.
Hang old rags on fence.
Spread tea towels on grass.
Pore wrench water in flower bed.
Scrub porch with hot soapy water.
Turn tubs upside down.

Go put on clean dress, smooth hair with hair combs.
Brew cup of tea,
Sit and rock a spell and count your blessings.

Anonymous

~10~

Photographer in Town

"Excuse me, Ma'am. You're standing in my light. Would you kindly step aside for a while?"

Beulah, who was hanging sheets, stopped in her tracks. She had one hand hanging on to the edge of a sheet, holding a wooden split clip-on pin, while her body stretched to reach the clothes line. Moses had strung some rope between the outhouse roof and the side of the chicken house, away from the back porch.

Prior to that, Beulah had hung the larger pieces of wash across the porch railing and on top of bushes in the yard to dry in the sunshine. But with constant blowing wind, she soon tired of fetching clothes that got carried away.

"Who are you and what are you doin' in our yard?"

"Ma'am. Thank you for moving, if you please." The man had his head buried inside a huge box with black curtains hanging all around it. He continued to stay inside the box for a few more minutes.

"Hey! I asked you who you are, and what's you doin' here. Can't you hear me?" Beulah came striding toward the box.

As if caught with his hand in the cookie jar, the dark-skinned man raised his head out of the hiding place.

"I'm James Presley Ball, Ma'am. From back east mainly." He smiled at Beulah through the longest and curliest black beard Beulah had ever seen on a man so young.

"That explains who you are, but you ain't told me what you're doin' on this property." Beulah stood with her feet planted squarely on the grass and her hands were clenched into tight fists. "Better speak up, Mister."

She heard him chuckle as he stared at Beulah through his beautiful huckleberry colored eyes. "I'm a professional photographer, Ma'am. Please call me James." He held out his hand but Beulah stayed where she was.

"I am photographing the entire west and I plan to spend a while in Helena, Montana Territory, recording anything and everything that depicts the way of life in this godforsaken, uncivilized place you obviously call home." He turned to look at the Fiske house.

"You own this house or are you the colored help." Disdain filled his voice and Beulah was offended by it.

"I *am* the housekeeper, if it's any of your business."

"No offense intended, ma'am. I am an abolitionist from Virginia and lived through the Civil War." He made a peace sign with his hands. "I was being rude. It's a bad habit I picked up as a young lad."

Beulah did not offer any information, except to tell Mr. Ball that she was a freedwoman, coming from Virginia hoping to open a school for colored children in the near future.

Mr. Ball pulled his arms behind his back and grabbed his hands.

"One of the reasons for my stopping over for a while is that there is a wonderful black community here. Why, you even have plans to build your own church just east of the main part of town, I hear." He apparently had done some sleuthing around and indicated that he was interested in the area.

Beulah eased the tension between them.

"Are you planning to film the blacks?"

"Yes, of course. My gallery in Ohio is filled with well over a hundred and fifty photographs and portraits of men and women and children and animals over a vast period of time, recording slavery, the war, the way of life for the blacks."

Mr. Ball motioned towards the front of the house where his wagon and team waited patiently for his return. The horse nickered and Beulah heard barking from inside the covered wagon.

"I walked toward the front door, Ma'am, when I noticed you in the sunlight and I wanted to capture you before the light changed. All it takes is a cloud overhead, or a few minutes of valuable daylight and the whole scene changes, sometimes lost forever." He put his hand on the black box as if touching an old friend. He stroked the length of the box. "You may come and look inside at the camera if you would like."

Beulah didn't budge. She stared at the platform on wheels that transported the box that held the camera. The whole contraption puzzled her. Mr. Ball could easily pull the camera yet it would be held securely in place when he wanted to stage a photo scene. It looked like a giant child's wagon, the tongue attached in such a way that it could be folded up and out of the way when the camera was being used.

"I am a freedman, myself. I have a studio and business with my brother in Cincinnati, Ohio. We have a very famous art gallery there and my daguerreotypes hang there for sale. Photographs of the west are in high demand. Many folks want to travel but distance, inconvenience, and the danger of coming into this unknown land hold them back." He shaded his eyes as he scanned the valley off to the north.

"I knew this would be a wonderful place to get scenes of the Prickly Pear Valley. Do you mind?"

Beulah was dumbfounded. "Well, why, I don't know. You'll have to ask Mrs. Fiske and she isn't home right now."

Just then the kitchen door flew open and several children of all ages bounded down the back steps spilling on to the grass. "Miss Roberts. Look! What is that?" A chorus of questions burst from their curious mouths. One of the boys walked all the way around the equipment. That looks very heavy. Is it?"

"Hello, children. I am a photographer. I take daguerreotypes. Stand in a row and I'll take your likeness." And, before Beulah or Sarah Marie could protest, Mr. Ball was back under the cover of the dark

64

heavy curtains. He twirled his box towards the children. Flame and little puffs of white smoke sparkled out of a funny looking T-shaped gadget he held in his left hand.

"That smells funny," said one of the Fiske children. They all watched as the breeze carried the smoke high into the air.

"There. All done." Out he popped. "You might have a glass of water to spare me?" One of the girls ran into the house and quickly returned with a mason jar full of cool water.

"Did I miss anything?" She looked squarely at the black man whose face was covered in curls as he gulped down the liquid.

"Ah! Just what I needed." He handed her back the empty glass. "Thank you, young lady." He turned to Beulah.

"I plan to return within the hour and speak to Mrs. Fiske about recording her beautiful house." He smiled. "I'll be taking myself and my wagon all around the town, so be watching for me." He waved as he pulled his platform toward the wagon in the yard.

Beulah did not see the photographer again at the house the rest of that week. She had mentioned the man and his intentions to Mrs. Fiske.

"My goodness, yes, he may photograph the house." Mrs. Fiske was all smiles. "I do hope he gives you ample time to get the housecleaning done before he returns." She looked about the social parlor. "You have been slacking off in your dusting. I can see particles in the air from over here."

"Yes, Ma'am. I'll see to it today." Beulah waited until Mrs. Fiske had left. She looked at the immaculately clean room. "Hhhmmph! Why, she can eat of fin that floor." Beulah walked into the kitchen and picked up her grocery list. She also pocketed a list for supplies for the clinic. *I've got errands to do and that sunshine is a callin' me outside.*

Beulah made her way down the dirt road, carrying a rather large hand-woven basket. She would be buying fresh vegetables from the Chinese Gardens.

Dr. Rodney and Dr. Amelia both used homeopathic means of healing in the Clinic. Certain herbs were available to them only through the Yee Wau Brothers Cabin and Chinese store. Other medicinals had to be ordered in and shipments were often late for deliveries. Beulah routinely checked to see that the supplies were in alphabetical order on the cabinet shelves when the doctors needed them.

As Beulah strolled past houses in various stages of construction, she thought about how rapidly the area was becoming a town. *In a couple of years, Helena will be the "Boston of the West." I'm a sure of it. I love being out here doin' my part to see that happen. Time sure is flyin' by for all of us, and Miss Amelia is so busy. I'm just burstin' inside with pride for what she's doin' for women strugglin' to survive out here.*

Beulah, still daydreaming, ran right into the photographer who had his head inside the black box. Her basket, filled with loose vegetables, spilled onto the street. "Oh! Oh! I am so sorry." Beulah tried to help Mr. Ball stand up and retrieve his dignity. "Let me help you."

Mr. Ball stood and stared at Beulah. "You needn't be so dramatic, young lady. A mere calling out my name would have sufficed." He smiled as he brushed off his pants at the knees. "Apology accepted. You'd be surprised how many times that happens to me. It's all in a day's work."

Beulah felt sheepish as she retrieved her vegetables to her basket. He was not injured, nor his equipment damaged. "Are you finding the subjects and information you seek?"

"There is so much here that I have rented a space in the vacant room on Last Chance Gulch in that building you can see from here." He pointed north to a brick front building. Beulah read "J.P. Ball—Photographer" that had been painted on to a swinging sign and hung from an anchor in the wood frame surrounding a window. "I plan to stay for at least six months. Maybe the changing of seasons will bring me some interesting photographs?" He chuckled.

"I've found many black cowboys dressed in western gear, carrying whips and firearms, and jackets made out of coyote hides with long fringe hanging from the sleeves." He pointed to his own sleeve, a black wool showing signs of wear and dust.

He frowned suddenly. "My wife is not really happy with me. But I have convinced her to follow me here. She will arrive in about two more weeks." He looked at Beulah. "I was thinking to call on you to help me welcome my Missus to Helena." He paused. "And, by the way, do you know of any houses for rent?"

Beulah laughed out loud. "You must be kiddin' me. A house to rent? Why, I've been chasin' that idea for over a year now. You might find a room to rent or an apartment over the laundry, or the Rodney Hotel. Good luck with that dream." *As far as meetin' your wife? Well, that remains to be seen.* She half-muttered to herself.

Beulah walked into the Yee Wau Cabin and savored the aromas that greeted her senses. "Good morning." She handed one of the Yee Wau brothers her list. "How are you?" Beulah spoke loudly and distinctly. Neither of the men spoke English. "When I open my school, maybe you will come and let me teach you some English?"

The man smiled, nodded and bowed. He scurried about the shelves and soon had everything Beulah requested. His fingers flew over the beads of the abacus and presented her with a total. "Fine. Put it on the tab for Dr. L. Rodney Pococke, M.D." This was common practice for Beulah. At the end of every month she presented a bill to the doctors for payment.

Beulah picked up her basket, stepped away from the counter and once again found her space filled with the photographer. "Do you always sneak up on people?"

"Excuse me, Ma'am. I wanted to tell you to be sure to look into the window at my store down the street. The photo I took of you hanging sheets is on display." He smiled, waved and went out the door before Beulah could catch her breath.

Now what is Mrs. Fiske going to think about this? Imagine that. Her sheets blowing in the wind for all of Helena to see. Beulah laughed until tears came. *Just the thought of that . . . my laws.*

Grandma Hicks
Photo by J. P. Ball

~11~

Chinese Community

"What's that noise? It sounds like gunshots!" The men shopping in the mercantile all moved as one body to the front door and ran out into the street. Mr. Mutchnik stood inside the doorframe.

"You men. Get back inside."

Another volley of shots filled the air with noise and acrid smells that were carried down Last Chance Gulch by the ever blowing wind.

Several men ducked back inside the store. Others ran up the gulch to investigate the shooting.

"You lads must be new to town." Mr. Mutchnik returned to his desk chair and spun around to face the group still standing by the door. "That shooting isn't gun shooting. It's the Chinese celebrating something today."

"What do you mean old man?" It's a celebration for the Chinese?"

Mr. Mutchnik walked over to a shelf and pulled down a bright red box.

"See this box? Why, it came up river about 4 days ago in a huge crate stamped "Made in China, Shipped from San Francisco, California, USA". He opened the red box, about the size of a woman's hat box, and reached inside to pull out a string of what looked like sausages all hooked together. Only it wasn't meat. The men stared. "That looks like . . . . like dynamite for the mines. Why you showin' us that?" One fellow with a definite Irish accent spoke out.

"Because *that* my friend, is what the Chinese call firecrackers." He passed around the string. "Be careful. It's dynamite. Each one of those little bags is a firecracker and when lit with a Lucifer they go 'B-A-N-G'. Got it?"

Before Mr. Mutchnik realized what was happening, he watched in horror as the last man in line grabbed hold of the string and ran outside with it. He reached into his vest pocket and pulled out a match stick and struck it on the post nearest the step railing. He held the flame near the firecrackers.

Almost instantly, and before the poor bloke could let go of the string, the firecracker burst into flames. Down the whole length of the string the bags exploded, the noise so loud that Mr. Mutchnik's ears were ringing.

Blood spurted everywhere and parts of the man's fingers flew through the air. "My God in Heaven. What has he done?" screamed a red-headed Irishman standing closest to the open door. Part of a thumb attached to the wrist bone landed with a thud on the porch steps. The chaos created a frenzy.

"Somebody get a rag to help this man. He's gunna bleed to death." They all turned to Mr. Mutchnik for help.

"There's a stack of rags by the side door there . . . right there." He pointed to the rag pile left for the men to wipe off their hands before walking among the shelves, handling the cans and equipment. "Who's got a horse and wagon here to take this man . . . ?"

Before he finished his sentence he heard a horse whinny as it pulled a wagon away from the building. The injured man, unconscious now, was dumped into the wagon box, his hand wrapped in old rags. The newly arrived Irishmen, still in shock, stayed near the porch afraid to move away from one another.

"I don't know what the doc can do about this one." Mr. Mutchnik shook his head in disbelief. In less than four minutes a man had lost his left hand, all because he was curious about the firecrackers and how they would explode.

"The Chinese use them all the time to chase away evil spirits and usually follow a funeral procession to keep the devil away from the coffin. They also shoot them off when they celebrate happy events in their community. We hear the noise all the time, coming from the south end of the gulch where they have their China town. I wonder if any of them ever get hurt."

Mr. Mutchnik told the strangers what he knew about the Chinese. Most had menial jobs at the mines. Some ran private businesses, such as laundries, near where they all lived in shared shacks. He knew they had their own medicine men, cooks, and a rank-and-file order that was religiously kept. Some were addicted to opium and rumors abounded about an opium den at the end of the street.

The Wong family clan ran a grocery store; the name always tickled Mr. Mutchnik. The sign outside the building read, "*Wing-Sheng Groceries*."

Sometimes Mr. Mutchnik wandered into the store and bought a few things just to be able to watch how Mr. Wong counted up the purchases on an abacus. He was faster pushing the little beads on the wire than most men could figure it in their heads.

Another favorite establishment that hired only Chinese men was the Yat Son Noodle Parlor. The restaurant was always full. Open 24 hours a day, the door never closed. The men working swing shifts in the mines could order a hot bowl of noodles, hard boiled eggs and Jasmine hot tea at any hour.

The south end of the gulch burst with activity. Vibrant colors were applied in the paint on the exterior of their buildings. The buttons and collars on the men's clothing, their language and polite mannerisms, all contributed to making Chinatown a curiosity for other ethnic peoples who wandered up and down the boardwalk.

Women who shopped at the butcher shop held their noses as they walked past the front window decorated with dead ducks, chickens, and rotting hunks of deer meat. Flies swarmed and landed on the carcasses. Occasionally, the onlooker wondered if maybe even some skinned-out dog and cat meat swung on huge hooks in that window.

The older Chinese, not able to work inside the mines any longer, worked the soil and produced hundreds of acres of vegetables for sale from late spring until after the fall harvest. Meeting a friend for a trip to the Chinese Gardens vegetable stand was a social event for the housekeepers of the high society women, often leading to a tea break in a local Chinese tea shop.

Beulah routinely shopped three times a week, sometimes more often depending upon the whims of Mrs. Fiske. During the social season, Beulah was called upon to make specialties for the hostess as she entertained the women married to the important leaders, the movers and shakers of the community.

The Chinese population rose into the thousands as Helena's unique opportunities for wealth reached China's shores. Letters written to those left at home spoke of great vision for future happiness.

The Chinese men held menial jobs alongside the Irish employed by the railroad that was being built on the west side of the Valley. Many were hard rock miners who knew how to blow away rock to spoon out tunnels through a mountain. The mine operators hired the Chinese men for pennies a day. Many lost their lives doing this dangerous work, only to be replaced within the hour by more men with big dreams.

Mr. Mutchnik, as a kindness, always accepted their freight orders when delivered into the town. He would then get word to Mr. Wong to come into his store and collect what they had ordered. Most of the men could not speak English. However, Mr. Wong spoke beautiful English, having been educated at a Christian school in his village at a young age.

Because of the poor economic conditions in China and the promise of finding mountains filled with gold, Mr. Wong had left his family behind. He planned to make a fortune in the mines and return to China to live out his life in luxury.

Mr. Mutchnik always enjoyed Mr. Wong's visits when he came into the mercantile. He secretly wished the little man much success. Many a time he watched him walk out the door. His black hair, gathered together at the nape of his neck in a long queue that hung down his back, was held tightly in place by a tight-fitting, brightly colored round silk embroidered cap.

With every visit Mr. Mutchnik was surprised to see he still had his hair. He'd heard stories about men ganging up on the Chinese men just to lop off their queues, thinking it sporting fun. He wanted to warn Mr. Wong of the pending danger but always held his tongue. His thoughts, however, he could not control.

I wonder how long he will have his queue. If he stays away from the cowboys in the bars on Saturday nights maybe he'll escape their capturing him and cutting off his gateway to heaven.

Yatson Chinese Food

Take time to laugh for it is the music of the soul.
Anonymous

~12~

The Irish

"Listen to that music. We can hear it all the way up the hill." Beulah and Amelia were standing outside the clinic at the top of Broadway Hill.

"It's the Seventeenth of March. I can tell you that without looking at the calendar." Amelia did a little Irish jig on the grass and both women laughed at how happy the music made them feel.

Sarah Marie and her school charges came rushing out the kitchen door and into the road. She waved at her sister and Beulah. Both women waved back.

"We're going to the parade. You better come along too." Sarah shouted over her shoulder as she passed by the ladies. "Once a year we get to usher in spring with good food, good green beer and great dancing."

"Amelia, if'en you want to go with them, I'll be here and will get word to you should you be needed."

"Thanks, Beulah, but you know there will be drinking and brawling in the bars in just a few hours and I best be prepared for it. Besides, we can hear the band from here." Amelia put her fingers in her ears and the women laughed with each other once again.

"Irish music does make one want to dance and feel happy, even when it's a sad, sad song that they'll be a playing soon enough."

Beulah thought about her southern gospel songs. "Surely it *is* different than what we grew up with, Missy, but I do enjoy listening to them play their tunes. Especially the tin whistles." She looked back towards the sounds. "I think every Irish lad in the world must have at least one tin whistle in his back pocket. They are made in large and small sizes."

Amelia sighed, as if deep in thought about the plight of the Irish.

"The Irish come to America with nothing but a song in their heart. They leave their poorest of the poor country hoping for a new start by finding gold nuggets in the streets after a heavy rainstorm." Amelia rubbed her left arm for a second. "Over and over I hear that story. They have been told in letters to join brothers and family in Montana Territory and so they continue to come."

Beulah nodded her head in agreement. "Butte seems to be their point of interest. After they get there, they fan out following the miners' dream, however misspent it may be. Word gets out fast when gold strikes are found in these mountains." Beulah turned her attention once more to the band music and started tapping her right foot.

"It *is* catchy and fun. I've been in the Irish pub, sitting in the "snug" visiting with other women a time or two.

Their stories go on and on. The séance' never gives the punch line until the very end if he is a good storyteller."

"Yes, but they always seem to end those pub outings with a "donnybrook" ending in an all-out brawl. I've seen enough broken noses, cracked ribs, and poked eyes since living here to last me a life time." Amelia clapped her hands together. "Well, I'd best be getting back inside and do some desk work. Let's just hope it will be a quiet night here at the clinic."

Sarah Marie and the children skipped down the hill to join the crowd gathered to listen to the Irish band. The laughter lit up faces throughout the groups forming on the street.

Loud comments from other ethnic ladies could be heard over the music. "We'll get to play our German band next month, wait and see." Then another voice raised a pitch higher. "We've got the best Scottish bagpipes this side of San Francisco," People laughed and shouted and hooted with each jibe, but today was Irish Day and the green won the attention of everyone in Helena.

The feeling of spring danced in the air. Hopefully the long dreary winter was behind them. If an occasional cold front moved through, at least there was the knowledge that it would not last more than a few days. The mines would soon be open and the mine bosses would be hiring. Money meant food and shoes for the children.

Yes, the Irish do it right. March 17th was a good day to be on the gulch listening to foot tapping, happy music that floated on the air taking the notes right to the throne of God.

It simply amazed Amelia how people moved around so easily and without the need for much in supplies. Most single men travelled by horseback or mule. Many walked hundreds of miles between towns for jobs. Very few travelled with families. That came later, after work and a place to live was secured.

Some men were in Helena for as long as ten years saving money, mailing it back to loved ones in Europe or Ireland. It was to pay for passage for wives and children waiting their turn to come to the Promised Land and find that gold in the mountains.

Their biggest barrier was language. Children learned quickly from each other, and took their new-found voices home to teach their parents simple words and phrases.

Beulah longed for the day she would be opening her school to teach reading and writing to all of the people mixing into America's melting pot.

The band shell had been decorated earlier in the day with green paper and ribbon tied together to make the structure look like a big fancy cupcake. Men in green uniforms, no uniforms, work clothes and wool suits, anything handy at the time, sat in wooden chairs, holding their various instruments. The whistles were in the front row, followed by brass instruments; violins filled in the rear chairs. An accordion player was off to one edge by the banister claiming he needed room to spread out his arms as he played.

Strains of songs that the crowd recognized filled the air for several hours. Children jumped to their feet and did jigs while adults tossed coins to them. They scurried like little mice picking up the coins hoping to gather more than their siblings.

Laughter and sunshine was a great combination for the Fiske children. Sarah Marie encouraged them to join in with the other children from the mine town. She knew too well that the miner's children did not mix well with the city dwelling children. Dr. Rodney and Amelia spent many hours tending to the miner's children in their mining camp homes. Their biggest problem was cleanliness. Lack of clean water and nutritious food claimed many a child with bad teeth and poor health often leading to early deaths.

Mrs. Fiske did not want her children exposed to illness, even though she herself went with the doctors to act as a nurse. She often put on teas and worked on committees to raise funds to be spent in the mining camps.

Many of the Irish men wandered out west after the Civil War and the defeat of several Irish Units. Their hero, General Thomas Francis Meagher encouraged the men to move. "The west is where the future for America lies." He would lecture in gathering halls filled with Irish from the slums of New York City. "Help me to populate this territory and we will have statehood. Jobs in all forms will be plentiful as buildings and houses will be necessary."

Thousands of Irish men followed like lemmings only to find that their leader had disappeared in the Missouri River on a dark July night. The newspaper reported that the acting governor had slipped from a boat deck and fell into the water. His body was never recovered and no one knew for sure what actually did happen. Many suspected he was murdered. He had not been popular in the political arena.

Bars lined the main street on both sides. The Central, Blue Moon, Buckhorn . . . all had a steady business. Higgins Bar advertised they were "Where Gentlemen Meet" and women were not allowed—period.

This day, however, the street fountains were filled with green water which delighted the children lucky enough to be lifted up for a taste by an older sibling or a stronger friend.

Many homes were celebrating with Irish ham baked in apple cider, and colcannon, (mashed potatoes with finely sliced cabbage mixed in) and the always present carrots. Every Irish household would have soda bread with the meal. Beer and lots of toasts would round out the evening festivities. Amelia thought of some toasts she had heard.

"The Irish man of the house always says to me, "God bless all who enter here," when I come for a medical call. "One night the patient died just a few minutes after I arrived and the woman of the house said, "May you be in heaven a half hour before the devil knows you're dead." Amelia smiled at that.

Beulah joined in with a remembrance of her own. "There was that time when we went to check on a child and the mother opened the door. She smiled at us and said, "You are as welcome as the flowers of May."

"We've been through so many new experiences on this path haven't we, Beulah? Are you happy being here?" She didn't wait for an answer. "I promise you, Beulah, we will get your school up and running maybe after the fall harvest this year. Wouldn't that be wonderful for everyone to learn English and to read and write? You would be adding to the future of this community with what you are eager to begin."

Beulah grew pensive. "Why Beulah did I embarrass you? I only spoke the truth." Amelia took Beulah's hands into her own. She held on to her friend only for a moment, but they both knew the friendship was sincere and they would be forever friends.

~13~

Virginia Farm

The fancy black buggy bumped over the ruts and potholes in the lane as the well-kept, matching pair of carriage horses pulled the real estate land grabber away from the Hicks farm outside of Port Royal, Virginia. The man, dressed in a white wool suit with a matching fur hat, probably ermine, leaned forward on the cushioned back seat, animatedly talking to his driver. The horses moved as if in a parade, their heads arched and feet prancing. Flies were out and obviously surrounding the carriage as the driver kept waving his whip across the flanks of the animals, not to force them to move faster, but to shield them from the bugs in the air.

Frank Hicks stood by the gate post, wondering what the outcome of their meeting this early morning would produce, hopefully, a quick sale.

Well, I'll know by the end of the week if the gentleman pays me what I'm askin' for this land. It's time for me to be headin' west and meet up with the family again.

He reached down and picked up a handful of soil. To walk away from his homeland was unthinkable two years ago, but now . . . well; loneliness for his family ties was strong, too. He let the red clay soil sift through his fingers and watched as the slight breeze carried it away to the other side of the lane. *I can farm on my own homesteaded land in Montana and be with my Mama and Pa in their old age.* Frank straightened his back. *I've got work to do. Guess I better start with feedin' the chickens.*

Feeding the chickens always brought a smile to Frank's face. He pictured his mama with her apron full of chicken feed broadcasting the seeds across the yard for the birds to flock around and peck at the ground for the rest of the morning.

He had been faithfully writing to his Pa. Plans were spelled out; a schedule of when Frank should plan to leave Virginia had been drawn up and a list of needed medical supplies sat on the kitchen table.

The last letter received from his Pa had specific instructions as to what to do with the farm animals, who to sell them to, and when to have a public auction for the machinery and household furniture. He would not be taking any items from the farm with him. He was to travel light, come up the Missouri River from St. Louis, and keep his money pinned tightly to his inside pocket. He had pondered the idea to pack up things for future use, but the cost to do so was prohibitive and there were no guarantees it would reach the destination.

One out of every three river boats sank as they journeyed up the Missouri River and freight had to be paid in advance. To take it overland meant finding drivers for wagons, and their demanded pay seemed way out of sight. Frank had enough saved for his own passage, and what he made off the farm sale would be sorely needed by his family to get him settled.

Good thing I still ain't married, he thought. *If 'en I was, I probably wouldn't be leavin' here.*

Moving west had been a dream of Frank's ever since the advent of the Civil War when all hell broke loose for Virginia and the Confederate Army. Hadn't his own brother seen to the fighting?

Best be getting' on with the chores. I'll take the auction posters to the post office and the mercantile store later this afternoon. The community board will come in handy for spreadin' the word about the auction sale. He looked about the fields and was sorry he had not planted crops this spring. *There's still time for the new owner to put in a hay crop in the first meadow and tobacco in the field across the way. But I won't be here ever again to see smoke comin' out of that old chimney Pa and I built ten summers ago for Mama's cookin'.*

Frank thought about the family and how content they all had been living here before the war. The idea came first to Grandpa Huntoon Hicks that they were going to leave the home for new land in the west. Then Pa and Mama and his younger brother George filed for homestead papers. They soon followed with their mule and wagons going overland.

They all thought Jeremiah Hicks had been killed fighting for the Confederate side of the Great War. Imagine Frank's surprise when he found Jeremiah hiding in the field . . . and he had a fellow soldier with him . . . Joseph Ward he called himself.

How many times have I read that letter from Jeremiah proclaiming his love for "Joseph" who really was "Josephine." His little brother all married up and a proud papa. To think they named their little fella after me. I guess they really did appreciate me givin' them my savins so's they could run to the west and start a new life.

By now Frank had reached the top of the lane and had entered the barn where the cow mooed a greeting. Frank stroked the old animal behind her huge ears.

"I'm gonna be takin' you down the road to the Miller farm in a few days, Bessie. You can keep givin' milk for that passel of young'uns' old man Miller has hangin' around."

As if understanding what was about to take place, the old cow moved toward the back of the stall, away from Frank. "Hey! You ain't makin' this any easier, gal." He chuckled out loud. *Here I am talking out loud to the animals.* Frank walked out of the barn and swiped his sleeve across his forehead.

The morning chores done, Frank headed for the kitchen. *After I eat I'll head for town. I need to clean up a bit before I go talkin' about gettin' a stage coach ticket. If I can, I'll go overland by stage to St. Louis and then up the Missouri. How long that will take? I'll find out today when I inquire about passage. Thirty-five days on the river, then by fall I'll be saying hello to my kin.* Frank smiled at that thought. *I'm ready to move on, but sure could use some help getting everything in selling condition. Maybe I'll ask around for some farm kid needin' some spendin' money.*

~14~

Frank Finds Josie

Josie had her head buried in invoices, matching them with orders received, when the bell tinkled as the door to the mercantile was pushed open. As usual, the wind rushed inside and her stack of papers flew about the desk top, some landing on the floor.

"Frankie Hicks! Quit playing with the door. Either stay in or go out." She got down on the floor to pick up the papers. "Come here, like a good little boy and help me pick up these papers." She scurried about this way and that, but came to a sudden stop when she ran into a pair of men's rather trail-worn boots.

The boots were attached to legs covered in Levi-Straus canvas pants. Josie sat back on her haunches, looked up and stared straight into the brightest blue eyes of her brother-in-law.

"Yes, Ma'am. Let me help you." The older man reached down to help Josie to her feet. "Well, I do declare. You can't be . . . Frank? Is it really you?"

"Yes, Ma'am. It's me, Frank Hicks all the way from Virginia."

Josie stretched out her arm and hand to shake his and he grabbed it, pulling Josie into a bear hug. The man smiled as he then held Josie at arm's length.

"Let me look at you. My brother was right. He wrote me you really filled out a dress in all the right places." His eyes twinkled as he continued to tease his sister-in-law. "I like you much better as a woman, Josie."

Josie blushed beet red and walked away from the man. "I received your letter about 6 months ago saying you were planning to come out west if the farm sold in Virginia. That must have happened sooner than you expected?"

Frank looked around for a chair to sit on and, not finding one pulled up an unopened barrel full of nails and plunked himself down. Josie returned to her desk chair, but kept her eyes glued to the man in front of her.

"Everything worked out better than I had imagined it would. I know I did the right thing by moving. The excitement of seeing family again grew with each day as I sold off equipment and gave away animals and stuff that I could not burden myself with on the trip." Frank looked around the building and noted how well equipped it was with farm implements, ropes, shovels, mining tools, household items. "I'm sure glad I didn't drag anything with me. It can be purchased right here."

Josie smiled brightly. "We have a very good inventory, Mr. Mutchnik; he was our landlord in St. Louis who came with his wife Mary, Jeremiah and me, keeps a good eye on the stock and is constantly reordering. Mary and I run the store. We take turns . . ."

Just then the side door swept open and in walked her son, Frankie.

Frank stared at the child, seeing the exact same resemblance of his dead brother, Jeremiah Hicks.

"Well, hello. So *you* are my namesake?" He ruffled the top of the child's head but did not try to hold him. Little Frankie ran to his mother and grabbed her skirt, but he turned sideways to look at this stranger who seemed to know him.

"Say hello, Frankie. This man has come a long way to meet you. "The youngster frowned. "You know me already? How come I don't know you?" His bright blue eyes, the same color as the tall stranger in farm clothes, grew large.

"Enough Frankie. Go find Mr. Mutchnik for me. Tell him we have company and to come to the store." Josie turned the child toward the door and gave him a little push. "Hurry, son. Tell Mary we have company for dinner, too."

"Please say you will stay and visit with us and take dinner tonight."

Josie brushed back her hair. "It's wonderful to see you again, Frank. There is so much to tell you about Jeremiah and me." She dropped her eyes and blinked back tears. This did not go unnoticed by the handsome man, older than Jeremiah but obviously a brother.

This time when the door blew open, Mr. Mutchnik had a firm hold on the doorknob. His presence filled the space. He looked surprised when he saw Frank Hicks sitting on a keg of nails talking with Josie as if it was the most normal thing to do. It upset him, this instant reminder of Jeremiah whom he loved like his own son.

"Welcome to Helena, young man." They shook hands before Mr. Mutchnik asked any questions. Josie knew there would be many asked at dinner, but for now she would keep the conversation light.

"Have you been to the homestead yet?"

He nodded. "Yes, Mama and Pa are both in fine shape and they have done wonders with the homestead. It is hard to believe so many years have passed since we have been together, and I know it makes them happy to have me out west now too." He kept his big rough hands on his knees as he talked.

"Did you come up river then?"

"I left St. Louis the first part of June, and in 42 days the boat tied up at Benton's Fort." Frank took a breath. "Then I rented a horse and saddle and got directions to find the Sweet Grass Hills and the homestead where my parents and other siblings are now calling 'home'."

Just then the bell rang from the front porch of the Mutchnik house.

"Mary must have dinner ready. Come son, you can wash up before we eat." Mr. Mutchnik motioned towards the side door. He twisted the lock on the front door; sure he would not be back to the shelves tonight.

Dinner, an aromatic beef stew with lots of carrots and onions and gravy, was perfect for the occasion of hostessing an unexpected guest. Earlier in the day Mary had made bread and since the oven was still hot, she'd decided to make a custard pie. Conversation was lively and fun once Josie got past the ordeal of telling Frank about the trip west. Out of respect and interest, he did not interrupt.

Mary kept a tight watch on the youngster, helping him cut his meat. She oversaw the bowls being passed around the table. Much of what Josie told Frank had also been kept secret from the Mutchniks all these past years, and Josie was allowed the time to tell her story in her own way, without questions.

There would be time for questions another day. Somehow, Mary instinctively knew that Josie and this stranger at their table would be linked in more ways than through the uncle-nephew relationship that existed between the man and the child.

I wonder if Josie sees Jeremiah when she looks at Frank or if he holds her interest in other ways. He's a very handsome man, and Josie has grieved long enough. I'm going to think about being a matchmaker very soon. If he stays in Helena long enough to get a few sparks going, anyway . . . . Lordy, Josie hasn't been courted in so long; she probably thinks it will never happen that she could fall in love. But here stands a perfect match for her. He's certainly interested, I can tell that by the way he keeps sipping his water and looking at her over the rim of the glass.

"There's a new hotel just down the main street called the Payne Brothers Hotel. They have a stable for your horse and they also serve breakfast, as well as other meals," spoke Mr. Mutchnik. "You'll be comfortable there . . . or nowhere." He actually laughed at his own joke.

~15~

Plans for Josie

Amelia stepped into the Mutchnik Mercantile and smiled when she saw Josie sitting at the high desk working her pencil on an invoice.

"Hello this fine day to you."

Josie, deep in thought, frowned when she saw Amelia. She still had not recovered from her recent discovery that Amelia was from Front Royal, Virginia and possibly knew her dead husband, Jeremiah.

"Yes, it *is* a fine day." She stood up from her chair. "What can I do for you? Are you shopping for something special?"

Amelia laughed and came further into the huge warehouse of a building.

"No. Actually, I came looking for you. Can you spare a few minutes to visit?" Amelia looked around the room and noticed they were alone, but for how long, she didn't know. "I've been meaning to come to you with some information about myself for a long time. The opportunity just never seemed to present itself and it bothers me to keep silent any longer."

Josie walked forward and motioned for Amelia to follow her. She picked up Frankie from his play area and the trio left the mercantile through the side door.

"Mrs. Mutchnik will come fill in for me. We can visit over a cup of hot tea inside the house." They crossed the yard and Frankie ran ahead to open the door.

"Grandma! He shouted through the door . . . company." Amelia saw Mary, who was looking through the window at the two women, and instinctively *knew* her secret was not a secret to these women.

"Water is hot. Come on in. Let's have us a good cup of Chamomile."

"How wonderful you look today, Mary. You are improving aren't you, both physically and emotionally from your accident."

Amelia walked over to the older woman and softly touched her hair, brushing back some strays that were showing definite signs of turning gray.

"Every month I see strength returning to my limbs, doctor. The movement is good for me and since the ramp has been in place, I can easily go from the house to the mercantile. I put in a shift every day there. Bookkeeping was always my suit in St. Louis and so it is here." Mary pushed her wheelchair with her feet and allowed the women to pass by her into the kitchen area where Amelia sat in a wooden ladder-back chair.

"My new wheelchair being built from my fantasy dreams will be ready for me in about two more weeks. I can hardly wait because with that new chair I'll be a free woman again, able to maneuver the boardwalks . . . at least the ones not built up on stilts." Mary smiled at Amelia. "To be able to go to Weinstein's Grocery Store is exciting. Frankie is strong enough and old enough to go with me and pull his red wagon and I'll fill it with purchases."

Josie looked away from Mary and rolled her eyes. Her actions revealing disapproval did not go unnoticed by Amelia.

"That IS wonderful news, Mary. I'll be waiting to see you rolling about town. Mr. Mutchnik better take out a patent on this contraption he is having built. After all, you drew up the plans. You will be the first to model it.'

Mary looked at the two younger women, tension mounting between them, and decided they needed privacy to discuss whatever had brought Amelia to her door this day.

"Speaking of that, I am going to take myself and Frankie back over to the store. Mr. Mutchnik is in the back room sorting the freight that came in yesterday. He's going to need to hire someone at the rate orders keep coming. This will be one busy summer. Come on, Frankie. Bye now."

Mary stopped for a moment. "Next time you come by be sure to bring your little son. He is always welcome in this house, you know." The door slammed shut behind Mary.

Josie poured the tea in ordinary cups. She set out spoons for the honey and a few cookies on a plate. "Have a cookie, Amelia." She pushed the plate in front of Amelia but did not take a cookie for herself. She sat waiting for Amelia to begin telling her what she already suspected from the information sent her by Frank Hicks.

"Josie, I have come to tell you about my past and it does include your deceased husband, Jeremiah." Amelia blew on the top of the cup, and then set it down on the table top. "We grew up in the same town, and went to school together. We were sweethearts in our teen years."

The napkin in Amelia's hand was being twisted into a long, narrow rope shape. "Before the war took Jeremiah away from me, I had big plans that we would attend college together and become man and wife." She reached up and dabbed at her eyes.

"Please, Amelia, don't . . ."

"Let me finish, Josie. I thought he was killed in the war and I went away to medical school in Boston. In the meantime, Jeremiah was serving for the Virginia Confederate Army. In a battle he apparently was wounded and that is when he met you." Amelia looked up and into the saddest eyes she'd ever seen as Josie listened politely.

"I met and married Dr. James Martin and we were truly in love with each other. When that deranged patient killed my husband I thought I would not survive another day without him." Amelia smiled a contemplative smile. As an afterthought, Amelia paused to form the right words.

"Josie, I did not marry Dr. Martin because Jeremiah was gone from my life. Our loving friendship was that of young teenagers who had no knowledge of the adult world."

Josie held up her hand to try to stop Amelia from continuing, but Amelia would not stop. "That is when I decided to come west with my sister and Beulah. Sarah Marie was looking for excitement and a new life; Beulah wanted to escape from the slavery issues still raging in the south."

"There was no correspondence between Jeremiah and myself. Nor did I know he would be in Helena. It never entered my head that I would find Jeremiah Hicks here. I was with child and had patients at the clinic to tend to and that comprised my whole world." Again she dabbed at her eyes ready to spill hot tears down her cheeks.

"When those men brought Jeremiah into the clinic for medical attention I was shocked and stunned. Then you came in and I recognized you and your baby from the boat we arrived on in Ft. Benton." Amelia looked at her hands, white knuckles showing the pain she felt telling this story out loud.

"I have gone over and over this, Josie. I wanted to find the right time to tell you, and then it just didn't seem to happen. I decided it should stay with the sleeping dogs, stay in the past, and so why dredge it up now."

Josie, quiet all this time, finally spoke. "Yes . . . why dredge it up now."

"Because, dear Josie, I want us to be forever friends. We have sons to raise, and we know people from our past that together put us into each other's way of life. We don't need secrets to push us away from a long and healthy friendship." Amelia took a sip of the tea, now cold.

"When my baby came right here in this house, it was your face I concentrated on. Your support at my time of need will remain etched in my heart forever. Please say you understand why I didn't tell you about Jeremiah."

Josie stood up and stretched. She turned her back on Amelia but spoke softly.

"I have suspected there was a connection but I didn't understand it all until a letter from Frank Hicks arrived last spring in March. In fact, I learned about your friendship the night your son was born." Slowly Josie turned to face Amelia.

"Thank you for telling me about your past. I figured it out that it was me Jeremiah loved and married . . . and I have his son to raise and love and remember him by." She rested her hands on the edge of the table and looked directly at Amelia. "Just do me one favor if you can."

"Anything, Josie just tell me what it is."

"Stop wearing that gold locket. It must have come from Jeremiah and when I see you that is all I see . . . that locket." She dropped her head down.

"We have not crossed paths too often this past winter, have we? I took off that locket and put it in a small box, locked it up and threw the key into the outhouse." Amelia took a deep breath. The memory still caused her deep pain. "Neither of us will ever see it again."

"Jeremiah promised me a wedding band when we got settled here. Mr. Mutchnik sold them in St. Louis, but I told Jeremiah not to buy one. We were going to wait until the Hicks family was all together and have a proper church ceremony." Now it was Josie's turn to dab at her tear-filled eyes.

"Amelia. We have too many memories holding us together like ties that bind. I *want* to be your forever friend. Now, let's put this behind us, raise our two boys in the eyes of God and follow the path of life given us."

The two women stood and hugged each other.

"I have news that I have not even told Mary." She looked rather sheepish. "Do you remember Frank Hicks? Yes, of course you do. Well, Frank sold the farm and has arrived here. He's courting me. We have a wonderful friendship that has turned the three of us into a family. We plan to marry very soon. He is Frankie's namesake and he will make me a good husband and be a wonderful father for Frankie." She looked straight into Amelia's smiling face.

"Mr. Mutchnik offered him a job in the mercantile business and we are seriously looking into a piece of land to homestead in the Wolf Creek area. Probably we will open a small general store where we settle."

Amelia grabbed the woman by her arms and they started dancing in circles around the kitchen floor. "Oh! What joy! How happy I am for you, Josie. You have every right to be with this man, for many reasons, and before long, there will be a sibling for Frankie." Then she grew pensive.

"You won't be moving before next spring will you?"

"Actually, I think we will probably marry this fall, very soon. Frank wants to take me to the Sweet Grass Homestead where his parents are and where his brothers are living and working their parcel of land."

"Wolf Creek isn't that far and we will be moving there by next spring, for sure, if we can get the homesteaded acres that Frank has been looking at."

"You will be travelling to Helena often?"

"I plan to be the postmistress there, just as I am here in Helena. So, yes, I will be riding the stage occasionally, and when I do we will spend time together." Josie tossed her head back and laughed so joyfully that Amelia found it infectious. The two women were laughing and crying at the same time when Mary came rolling through the kitchen door.

"What's all the noise about in here? Can I join the party?"

Josie rushed to hold open the door so Mary could wheel herself comfortably into the kitchen. She had rolled up sheets of paper across her lap.

"I've brought the house plans to show you Dr. Amelia. We have the foundation in, as you are aware, but these plans will show you how our mansion is going to look on the west side of Helena. The same contractor who is building the Ming Mansion is going to oversee the working crew on ours and we will be neighbors. There are places for gardens and the first thing I am going to have done is plant an apple tree and a lilac bush."

Dr. Martin spread the plans on the table top and stared at the beautiful designs.

'This is magnificent. I see you are building out upon the landscape instead of up into the air. You don't need steps, Mary. Remember to be firm and strong about no steps when the men try to change your mind about room spaces."

"Mr. Mutchnik and I have discussed that very thing. He is getting older, too, and is satisfied with a one story house with lots of rooms. We will have an office, dining room, inside kitchen, washing area for the cook and a play area for Frankie, along with four bedrooms. We will need many fireplaces." Mary clapped her hands in pure excitement at the very idea of starting the construction in just a few weeks.

"We have the money to build what we want and need. Mr. Mutchnik will see to it that only the best supplies will be used in this house. It will still be here one hundred years from now. Maybe Frankie will live in it with his wife and family."

Josie looked at Amelia, then at Mary. "I think we have all kinds of things to celebrate this afternoon, and this new house is just perfect for my future plans, too, Mary." Josie walked over to Mary and put her arms around the older woman's shoulders. "I have news of my own."

Mary waited, anticipating what Josie was about to say. "Out with it girl."

"You know I have been seeing a lot of Mr. Hicks this past summer. Well, he has asked me to marry him and I said yes. We want to wed in the fall. I plan to move to where the homestead is for the Hicks family and we will be trying to get our own land in the Wolf Creek area as soon as the government releases it."

Mary sat very still and did not try to stop the tears that spilled down her cheeks.

"I don't know whether to laugh or to cry, Josie. But I am happy for you and for little Frankie. He needs a father and who better than Mr. Hicks?" She put her hands together and Amelia noticed her knuckles were white since she held them so tight. "Maybe we will have the house and yard in order before you wed? Would you like to have the ceremony at our new house with a reception in the yard?"

Amelia looked at Josie and waited for her answer.

"I'll have to ask Frank about that, Mary. We are going to take a trip to visit his parents and had talked about my moving with him and marrying there." She dropped her voice to a whisper. "How can we all be together in separate places? I can't do that to you and Mr. Mutchnik, you mean too much to me." Josie ran out of the kitchen.

"Let her go, Mary. This is a big decision only Josie and Frank can make. How they begin their wedded life is their choice. We can hire a stage coach and all of us attend the wedding. We can stay in Ft. Benton. A vacation will be good for all of us."

Amelia knew she was talking to deaf ears. There was time to go over making plans for the trip to the wedding as summer wore on. She would be there to support Josie and Mary any way she could.

Amelia walked into the parlor where she found Josie looking out the front window of the little shack of a house she called home for a couple of years. It would not be easy for her to move little Frankie to a new location, but her love for Frank Hicks was deep and true, comfortable, and just right for her son and for her. She would be strong for everyone and it would work out as the season wore on.

"I am leaving now, Josie. I must get back to my little Joseph and to the clinic."

She tugged at her reticule, pulled out a pair of gloves, straightened her feathered cap, and waved goodbye to little Frankie who was playing with wooden blocks in the very room Amelia had given birth to her little boy just a few short months ago.

My goodness but life certainly tosses in surprises. This is going to be an interesting summer. I half expect Sarah Marie will be making her own announcement one of these days. But she is still very young and Mr. Frey can see that in her. I'll have to have a talk with my little sister one of these days. And then there is Beulah. What is to become of her? That will be another talk one day soon.

Amelia walked briskly up the boardwalks that kept her skirts out of the dust. *For that matter, what is my future here in this mining camp and what about Joseph's future?*

I love living here and there is plenty of activity if one wants to get involved. Time . . . oh precious time . . . you do heal wounds. Too bad you leave jagged stitches in the process.

~16~

Proposal

Sarah Marie walked with purpose, head held high. She did not see the wagon parked off to the side hidden in the shade of the huge cottonwood tree.

"Hello, pretty lady. Care to have some company this lovely afternoon?"

Sarah Marie stopped at the sound of the now very familiar voice.

"Why, Mr. Frey. How nice to see you on this beautiful spring day." She curtsied and opened her ever present fan that dangled from her wrist, and flirted with her eyes. "I would, indeed, enjoy your company. I am feeling a bit abandoned, to be honest." She stepped very close to the cowboy and he reached for her right arm near the elbow.

"If you walk with me to our house, I'll treat you to lemonade and cookies."

"How can I resist such a tempting offer?" He stepped to match her stride. "I have something to discuss with you, Sarah Marie. I am glad to find you alone for a change."

Sarah Marie was instantly alert to the tremor in his voice and wondered what he had to tell her. *Is he ill? Maybe leaving the ranch? Taking another job, or going into the mine fields by Marysville?*

"Why, Mr. Frey, you can tell me anything." She pulled open the wrought iron gate and gracefully stepped through while the cowboy waited his turn to enter.

"Come, sit on the porch. I'll be just a minute in the kitchen and then I'll join you." She smiled. "Isn't this just a perfect spring day? There is no cold wind blowing from the mountains. I do hope we see a robin very soon so the spring season will officially be upon us." *Why am I babbling like a school girl?*

Wicker chairs stood on either side of a small wooden table. Sarah Marie hurried to pour two clear crystal glasses of lemonade made earlier and served with lunch. She put four cookies on a lovely plate decorated with a hand-painted pink rose. The signature of an unknown artist from Germany, plus a green crown emblem embossed the underside. This plate was used only for special occasions. Sarah Marie wanted to serve her guest in style and she would be very careful to see that nothing happened to it. She hurried back outside to the waiting cowboy.

"Here you are, sir." She handed him the glass. "Now, what is it you wanted to talk to me about?" She sat in the chair opposite him.

"Sarah Marie, I have been courting you now off and on for a few years, waiting for you to grow up."

Sarah Marie stood straight in her chair. "Why whatever do you mean, "grow up?" I am 21 years of age,

I'll have you know." She bristled at his words. I've been teaching school for five years and . . ."

"Well, yes ma'am," he interrupted, but you were only a very young woman when you first arrived." He took a big gulp of lemonade. "This is not going well." He paused. "Please, let me start over."

Sarah Marie settled back into her pillow on the chair and smiled. "As long as you are not trying to tell me you are leaving the area or something worse, I guess you can start over."

The cowboy stared at her. "Whatever gave you that idea?" He took a breath, then blurted, "Sarah Marie, you are the strangest creature I have ever met."

"I am what?" Sarah Marie jumped to her feet. "What on earth is wrong with you? You are shaking, saying weird things about me, and not making any sense."

"Maybe you better leave and come back when you are ready to tell me what it is that is bothering you." Sarah Marie remained standing but to her surprise, her cowboy slipped out of his chair and knelt on one knee. He reached for her hand.

"Sarah Marie Roberts, I love you and have from the first time I saw you at the river's edge in Fort Benton. Will you marry me?"

"Well, I never . . . marry you? She paused as if deep in thought. "I thought you would never ask." Sarah Marie gripped the young man's hand and pulled him to his feet. "Marry you? I would be so honored to be your wife." She smiled into his eyes and watched as the worried look left his countenance to be replaced with an ear-to-ear smile.

"Yippee! She said YES!" The only other living creature nearby was the mongrel dog that had adopted Sarah Marie before winter had set in. He barked and jumped around the couple as the cowboy swung his lady around and around on the porch. "Set me down before the neighbors see us." She brushed at her skirt. "I'd like to be married in October . . . if that fits your job schedules for ranching."

"Whenever you want to tie the knot is fine with me. The harvest will be in, cattle sorted for winter pasture, and it would be a better time and season for me at the ranch."

"Then it's settled. I'll start making plans for an October wedding here in Helena."

All kinds of questions filled Sarah Marie's head and she spoke easily about them. "Where will we live?? Is there a ranch house for hired hands with a new bride?" She looked up at her love.

"We might live that first winter here in Helena, but I'll continue working on the ranch. Hmmm! Jack Frey married. I like that idea . . . like it a whole lot." He smiled at his new fiancé.

"Yes, we will have our own house, not the bunk house. I'll see to that right away, even if I have to build it myself this summer. Nothing fancy right away, but we'll work towards having a spread of our own somewhere around Wolf Creek. I've applied for homestead acres already and it will take a while to get the government to answer."

"I've waited for so long to hear you propose to me. Why the thought of marrying a rich cowboy is what enticed me to come west long before my sister planned to do so."

The cowboy tipped back his hat and laughed until he had tears in his eyes.

"Only one thing wrong with your plans, sweetheart. Cowboys are hired hands and none of us is rich. The ranch owner gives a fair wage, and I've been saving most of mine." He very proudly continued talking. "Someday we'll have a homestead and our own place."

Once again he pulled his future bride close to him. Sarah Marie laid her head on his chest and felt the pounding of his heart. "We'll be a good team, you and me." His voice was soft and tender as he kissed her right there in front of God and the neighbors. She did not protest as he continued to hold her in a tight embrace.

Suddenly she started to giggle. "Have you ever heard the poem that says,

"Don't kiss out by the garden gate. Love is blind but the neighbors' aint?"

Mr. and Mrs. Jack Frey

~17~

Two Weddings in Town

Sarah Marie spent the summer months preparing for her wedding to be held on October Sixth, at the Interdenominational Church built for multi-purpose use. Anyone who wanted to rent the space could do so by giving a donation for the building maintenance.

Since her fiancé, Jack Frey, did not have relatives in the area, they decided to make a public announcement about a month in advance and hang a notice on the post office bulletin board. This was a common practice in the community and many friends would pass the word that they were invited to the upcoming nuptials.

Sarah Marie understood why her mother and father would not be present and it saddened her when she compared her wedding day to that of Amelia's held in their rose garden in their home in Virginia.

What is . . . just is. She let her thoughts wander for a few minutes back to that happy time so many years ago now. She wanted to marry her cowboy and live in the west and that was going to come true in just a few short months.

Cookies, punch, little fancy edged sandwiches, coffee, tea and wedding cake would be served. Sarah Marie had already asked the Fiske children to be her helpers at the wedding and at the reception. Amelia would be her Matron of Honor, and one of the cowboys who worked with Jack would stand up as the Best Man. Plans were to be kept simple, but festive. Sarah Marie would see that some decorations would be in place. A wreath on the church door with ribbon streamers was already made and stored in a box in the empty bedroom of the cottage. The Fiske girls would wear wreathes with the matching ribbon streamers on their heads.

A friend of Sarah Marie's who worked at the local bakery had asked to bake the cakes, one a fruit cake for Jack and the men that she had secretly already made, and wrapped in cheese cloth, soaking in rum.

The bride's cake would be two white layers made from the new Gold Medal Flour that had won all the prizes at the World's Fair. The frosting would be whipped cream with berries floating across the top. She had preserved the strawberries and raspberries all during the summer months to be sure and have a supply when it came time to decorate the wedding cake. It would be a fancy, memorable cake, setting the mood for the reception.

Sarah Marie designed her own dress. She and Josie studied materials available, and one session finally brought a smile to Sarah Marie's otherwise frowning face.

"There." She pointed to a picture of an ivory paisley material that curled every which way and gave off a shimmer even noticeable in the Sears catalog. "That will make a beautiful wedding dress, and I'll be able to wear it for other occasions for years to come." She wrote down the catalog number on an order form that Josie had handed her when they first started searching for materials.

"I want to be able to make mutton sleeves, and a bell skirt, and I know lace is so very expensive and rather hard to find, but I do want some lace around the collar and cuffs."

"Let's keep looking. We'll find it. What about your hair? Do you want a crown with pearls and a long veil?" Josie and Sarah Marie looked at each other and laughed.

I hardly think so. I was thinking more of an off white fitted cap with a white feather and maybe an ivory loop of ribbon shaped like a flower?"

"The lady who just started her millinery shop on Last Chance Gulch can do that for you. I'll ask her when she comes in to pick up her order this afternoon."

"I'll need a pair of nice high buttoned shoes, too." Sarah Marie put down her pencil. "I hate to spend money on white shoes when I know I will be wearing work shoes the next day." She rubbed her forearm for a minute as if in deep thought.

"But, it is my wedding day. I can borrow Amelia's white ballerina slippers that she wore on her wedding day." She sighed. "Yes, I will write Mother this afternoon and you can post it from here. Mother will send them to me."

"I'll get your order right out today as it will take a while for this material to come from St. Louis. It will be at least a month coming up river, but we do have time." Josie made some notes.

"You know what, Sarah Marie?" I like everything you have planned for your wedding and you know I am getting married in October to Frank. We will be married in Sweet Grass where his family lives." She smiled at the thought of her own wedding.

"Why don't we share the expense of the dress and shoes and both wear the same clothes? No one will notice because the guests will be different at each wedding."

Sarah Marie, at first was taken by surprise by the idea, but then softened to the proposal. "That is a wonderful idea, Josie. We are about the same size and we can make alterations if need be on the dress. Oh! Be sure to order double ribbons, though as the girls will want to keep their headwear as a souvenir of the wedding."

Both women smiled, shook hands on their agreement, and parted to continue on with their individual day's activities. Josie busily prepared the order form so it would not delay the postal rider when he came by later in the day.

Jeremiah and I were to be wed proper with his family around us. Life certainly has a way of fooling people. Here I am a widow with a little boy, and I am about to marry my brother-in-law. How fast my life changed directions. I never dreamed I'd be out west seven years ago when I was fighting in the Civil War and met Jeremiah.

Tom Cruise was a lonely man. He achieved his goal of coming to the west from Ireland and finding the mother lode in a mine at Marysville, several miles to the west of Helena; A mine that would pay out a fortune to the owners for over a hundred years, he was sure of it.

Now it was time to find a bride. He had met and was attracted to Margaret Carter, the legal age daughter of Senator T. Carter. Margaret had accompanied her father to the Cruise mansion on Helena's west side for many formal occasions.

I will court her and see where this leads. Oh! What am I thinking? I am an old, broken down Irishman. What would she see in me? Well, there is no harm in asking her if she is interested.

The wedding of the century was planned for the same day as Sarah Marie's wedding day. The Cruise-Carter wedding, however, would not overshadow Sarah Marie's day. The Sacred Heart Catholic Cathedral on the hill would peal out wedding bells from its bell tower. Flowers would be freighted in, as well as scrumptious foods from San Francisco, Chicago, and New York; Parisian cooks were already arriving, even though the wedding was months away. Every hotel room had been booked and paid for in advance, with Mr. Cruse picking up the tabs in every bar in town for that day. The water fountains on the street corners were to be filled with champagne for the day. Nothing was to be spared to make this the most elegant affair to be remembered for years to come.

Special engraved invitations were being turned out on satin material at a printing shop in New York City. These would be hand delivered to special friends.

"I will pay for everything for twenty-four hours and give the people one fine time. But that will be a one-time event and I will not donate to any other causes ever again." Cruse shook hands with each bar owner as he made the arrangements up and down the gulch.

The Carter family was happy for Margaret. She would want for nothing the rest of her life. On her wedding day she was to receive one million dollars as a gift from her new husband. Every child conceived would also receive one million dollars at birth. And, as if that was not enough of a nuptial arrangement, Cruse gave Senator Carter one million dollars for allowing his daughter to marry him, a man who could neither read nor write and barely spoke English.

Both weddings took place as planned. Sarah Marie's reception held in the church hall with 20 family and friends gathered to wish her and Jack a happy life. Her gifts were all useful items for their homesteading plans; a quilt with the log cabin pattern had been neatly folded over the backs of two wooden chairs so the women could "ooh and aw" at the beauty of the intricate spread made from scraps cut from worn out shirts, dresses and fancy flour sacks.

The lilac bushes stood clumped together in a wooden bucket for planting at their soon-to-be homestead. Sarah Marie opened the attached card. "Oh, look Jack . . . read out loud what Mrs. Sanderson from Augusta wrote to us."

Jack lifted the card and read. "Remember, after you plant these lilac bushes from my yard, and they bloom, spreading the most wonderful perfume into the air, that in three weeks your hay will be ready for harvest." Everyone in the room laughed as they crowded around watching the opening of the presents.

Jack lifted one bush then the other. I wonder how big these will be when we finally do get that piece of land. Anybody want to place bets?" Again there was happy laughter and the women guffawed at the idea of a bet.

"Open mine next, please," said Mrs. Fiske. "The girls and I made this especially for you to remember us by." The girls curtsied and giggled while Sarah Marie carefully tore the brown paper from the large square package.

Much to Sarah Marie's surprise, she found herself staring at the girls hair-curls shaped like flowers and glued inside a rather ornate gold frame. The golden shades of blonde, and light tan, had been carefully saved during a recent hair cutting session, and the darker colors were used for stems and leaves. "Why, this is breathtaking." Sarah Marie smiled at the girls who were obviously so pleased with their gift. "We will hang it on our hall wall. You will have to come and visit us one day next summer when school is out." Sarah Marie walked to the girls and ruffled each head of hair.

Another stand-out present was Beulah's gift. She had sent away for a very fine book with real gold writing stamped on the cover. Sarah Marie wiped a tear as she read, "Holy Bible" and flipped open the book to the last page. There she recognized Beulah's hand writing. The date, year, and place had been neatly written on the top line of the "Family" page.

Other presents included much needed kitchen items like mixing bowls, handmade knives and spoons and forks. Dishtowels and pillow cases hand-stitched with sampler alphabet designs, days of the week ditties and pink roses would be used every day. Flour sacks cut and stitched into aprons completed the gifts. The gifts came from resources available to the women and every one of them had a purpose for her future life as a pioneer bride on a homestead.

One of the ladies from the church kitchen shouted out from behind the counter, "Now let us gather over here and eat these lovely cakes." She held up a small white box. "Anyone wanting to take home a piece of wedding cake be sure to put it into the little white box on the end of the table here. We all want to have pleasant dreams tonight, don't we?" Giggles from the little girls warmed the hearts of the congregation.

"We want to thank each and every one of you for coming to help us celebrate our wedding day," spoke Jack as he stood next to Sarah Marie. "We'll be living in town through this winter, but hopefully, next spring we'll hear about our bid for a homestead north of here." He made a gesture toward the stacks of gifts. "Everything you have given us today will be used 'til it falls apart, you can be sure of that."

He waved as he pulled Sarah Marie towards the door. "Stay as long as you like and enjoy the coffee and cake, but I've got a surprise for Sarah Marie and we have to leave now."

Naturally, the crowd followed outside. There they saw the farm wagon all dressed up in floral wreaths. Even the horses wore wreathes and ribbons around their necks. One stomped his front feet, anxious to get on the road.

Sarah Marie looked bewildered as she sat on the front board. From out of the crowd, someone tossed rice and another tossed flower petals. Down the road and out of sight went the newlyweds, destination unknown.

"Anyone want to make a bet they are goin' to Great Falls?" A few of the women slapped their menfolk on their arms and marched back into the church hall for another round of delicious cake.

Beulah, always in charge, welcomed them all back inside. She carried a hot tea pot in one hand covered by her apron front. She looked around the hall for Amelia and found her rocking her son; both were tired out from the day's festivities.

Amelia caught her searching for her with her eyes. "Well, my little sister has finally met her match in Jack Frey." She mouthed the words that only Beulah heard as the rocker continued to sooth the tired little boy.

Across town at the Sacred Heart Cathedral, hundreds of friends and dignitaries of Thomas Cruse stood in formal black tux dress and top hats. The women, wearing their finest sparkling jewels, modeled their fox fur capes covering special evening gowns. The late afternoon wedding ceremony had taken over an hour and it felt good to be outside in the fresh autumn air.

A ball of magnificent proportions was about to begin. Several men carrying musical instruments had been spotted entering the Grand Central Hotel where the top floor was their destination. A bandstand at the far end of the cavernous hall would provide seating for the musicians and they were to play continuously all evening. Tables decorated with floral arrangements and white circular table clothes lined the walls on the other three sides of the room.

One floor had been set aside with tables laden with wedding gifts, and a guard stood at the main doorway so that only those with invitations could attend the festivities. Family and friends crowded into the building, anxious to view the beautiful decorations and festoons. They were handed fluted champagne glasses as they entered the dining area off the first floor.

Thomas and Margaret would attend for one hour, and then they planned to slip away quietly. They had tickets for a trip to Paris leaving from New York City. The Northern Pacific Railroad left for the East that very day and it would not leave without the newlyweds. Their luggage was already at the station.

"It will take a while for this town to settle back to normal after today," said Josie to Frank as they strolled along the boardwalk on Last Chance Gulch. Little Frankie skipped ahead of them by a few paces.

"I hope our wedding is a simple but festive day," said Frank.

"Oh it will be. In just two more weeks we will be traveling to Ft. Benton and on to the Sweet Grass Hills." Josie reached for little Frankie's hand as they neared the hotel where the people gathered to enter.

~18~

Five Years Later

Sarah Marie stood at the edge of the iron fence that surrounded the small cottage she had shared with Amelia before marrying her cowboy. Swollen eyes could not hide the sadness and the tears that she had spilled over the past several days. She thought her heart was going to break when Amelia told her of her decision to return to Virginia.

"Why, Amelia? Why? You *love* it out here . . . at least *I thought* you did. You have always seemed so happy with your practice and with the help you have provided for women."

"Dear sister, I know this is upsetting to you, but it is something that has been on my mind and heart ever since we received the letter from Mother telling us that Father suffered a massive heart attack and died last year. We didn't even know it had occurred and Mother faced all of her grief without her daughters to comfort her."

"Then just go for a visit and stay a few months before you decide to make a permanent move. Mother could come out west, couldn't she?" Sarah Marie took her sister's hand into hers. "Please give me that much. Take Joseph James back to meet his grandmother. Have Beulah renew ties with her family." She paused in thought. "Why, maybe you can convince those brothers of ours to come west and we would be a family here in Montana Territory." More tears spilled down her cheeks but she made no attempt to wipe them away.

"Since Father passed over, the village is without a doctor. It might be that I am needed there rather than here. After all, we have Maria Dean along with the lady doctor who just moved into Marysville to help the miners and their children when illness strikes them. And Dr. Rodney's nephew is doing a great job right here in the clinic." She smiled about that. "I wasn't too happy about his arrival and felt crowded, but he is very well accepted and he is a knowledgeable physician." Amelia sighed.

"Sarah Marie, go home to your husband and your little girl. Everything is going to work out the way it is meant to be on this journey called 'life'." She smiled. "Joseph James, Beulah and I will be leaving next stage out, which is only a few days away." She took a breath. "It is not that I have never mentioned this possibility of my leaving to you, and my decision has been made."

"Have you explained all of this to Joseph James? Does he understand he will be moving permanently away from the only home he knows?"

"Now, Sarah Marie. You know I have told him about the trip to see his Grandmother. I will gradually tell him we are staying with Grandmother over the summer months. Then in the fall I plan to enroll him into the private school in the village that you and I attended when we were children. It is important to me that he gets a good education." She looked upon her sister with fondness and smiled.

"Please, don't be crying like this in front of the child. It will only confuse him." Amelia walked away from Sarah Marie and up the walkway to the house she had purchased when the family who had built it several years earlier had decided to return to Ohio. She did not want Sarah Marie to witness her tears. *Maybe there is something in this house that makes people want to return to their roots?* Amelia shook her head to clear it. *No matter. My decision is final. We leave on the stage in a few days. Beulah can return if that is her choice to do so. She has told me she plans to talk her brother Rufus into coming back with her. We shall see if that happens. Good luck for them both if that is their decision.*

The days were filled with choosing proper clothing and packing belongings into trunks to be freighted back east. Amelia planned to only take one travel-size valise for her and a smaller leather carrying case for the boy's clothes, along with some toys and books. These would accompany them on the river boat.

Before she had a chance to change her mind about leaving, tickets were purchased and the larger trunks delivered to the freight office. These trunks would not be on the stage with passengers but would arrive separately at a later date. She intended to go up river out of Fort Benton on the Missouri River. The freight would be transported overland.

The early morning hours brought Sarah Marie, Jack and their infant daughter to the cottage. They were to escort Amelia, Beulah and Joseph to the stage station. The trio stood at the fence, filled with mixed emotions.

"It was here in this gulch that I healed, Sarah Marie. And someday I will bring Joseph James back to his birth place and to you. Be happy, write as often as you can, and . . . soon the railroad will be complete from coast to coast and you can come visit us."

Sarah Marie held a handkerchief to her eyes and dabbed back the tears ready to spill over the surface. "Yes, I promise to save every penny from the egg business I am starting this spring." She threw her arms around Amelia. "This might be the last time I see you. I can't let you go."

Amelia smiled at her younger sister. "You always have been the dramatic one. You have a dream of your own to fulfill. Get that homestead livable and have more babies. Life is full of adventure for you." Amelia kissed her sister on her cheek and tasted salty tears.

She grabbed on to her son's hand and the procession continued down the boardwalk to the waiting wagon where Jack Frey would once again gave the sisters a ride. "I'm always here for the likes of you two. From bringing your luggage to Helena from Ft. Benton, to being there the night your son came into this world, to marrying Sarah Marie. Now here we are, full circle. I wonder how come?"

Sarah Marie fell into his waiting arms. He helped them all into the buckboard and drove slowly to the stage station.

Amelia held her son's hand and directed him toward the stage. "Look at how big this stagecoach is, Joseph. We are going for a long ride in it today."

Joseph pulled away from his mother and ran to Sarah Marie, wrapping his arms around her hips. "Why aren't you coming with us?" His eyes were wide and round as he looked at his aunty. He had never been apart from her and he thought of her as his second mother. For several years he did call her "Mama" and loved it when she'd sing him to sleep on nights his mother was out on a medical call.

"Come along, Joseph. The stage is waiting for us to board." His mother smiled as she gave her five-year-old son a scoot on his behind. The little boy hopped up onto the dropped-down iron step to enter the carriage. He turned around saw the people waiting in line. Beulah was next to step on board, waiting for Amelia to find her cushioned leather seat.

"Where are we going exactly? Is it very far away from Auntie Sarah Marie? Joseph was reluctant to sit in the coach. "I think I want to stay here."

Amelia sighed. "We've talked about this, Joseph. We are going to visit your grandmother in Virginia. It's a long ways away and you have to be a very good child for Beulah, so you don't get lost from us." Amelia rubbed her hand across her forehead.

Two days ago she had decided to wear a light green, wool two-piece skirt, blouse and jacket. It fit her well and required no extra underclothing or hoops so as to not take up space needed in the coach for other travelers.

She decided on a perky pillbox style hat with a matching plume on the right side of her head. The feather fluttered in the breeze and Amelia now questioned her choice for hair covering.

Beulah sat on the opposite side of Amelia, next to Joseph. She, too, wore travel clothes that were easy to care for along the journey. Hidden pockets inside the skirt held money, jewelry and documents. She decided on a light weight veil for a hair covering. She could put it around her shoulders like a shawl or keep her head covered from wind if necessary.

"Why are we going to visit my grandmother?"

"Your grandmother wants to meet you." Amelia pushed her fingers through the boy's curly hair. "She wants to hug you and kiss your rosy cheeks, and feed you cookies." She rested her hand on the boy's shoulder, feeling through his shirt how muscular he was for his age. "It has been six years since I have seen her, too. Your grandmother is *my* mother." The child looked confused. "Yes, it is true." Amelia chuckled. "I have a mother even though I *am* all grown up."

Joseph shook his head and snuggled in tight next to Beulah. "No, no. No kisses. Ugh!" Beulah put her arm around the little fellow, and then started tickling his ribs. "You just wait until *my* mama gets ahold of you, too." Joseph stared up at her, thoroughly confused that now even Beulah had a mother.

Amelia sighed. She blinked her eyes tight to hold back tears. Her father would not be in the depot waiting for their arrival. *It will be very strange to go home and not have father in the clinic. Poor mother having to deal with his death.*

"I don't like wearing this jacket and short pants, Mother." Joseph squirmed in his unfamiliar clothes. "Can I take off the jacket now?" Beulah reached over to help him shrug out of the jacket. "Now you sit still. Soon there will be things to see out the window."

Beulah sat back in the pillows. She knew as soon as the horses started pulling the coach it would be a bumpy, long ride, an endurance race all the way to Fort Benton. Amelia had paid a premium price of $15.00 each for two window seats and $10.00 for Joseph to have the middle seat. That way he could move around between the two women, sleep on their lap or be read to.

Once there, the paddle-wheeler, flat-bottomed boat, would be much more enjoyable for Joseph. He would be free to walk around the deck, and have comforts, like a cot to sleep on, and toys to keep him occupied. He would enjoy watching the river bank where animals and wild Indians eyed the boat as it passed by them winding its way to St. Louis, Missouri.

When the last letter from their mother, framed in black ink, had arrived for Amelia and Sarah Marie, Amelia made immediate plans to return for the visit. Never had she felt as helpless as when she read the news that their father had suffered a massive heart attack and collapsed in death.

After Amelia had stuffed their lunch basket under her feet, she studied her son's face. *How much he looks like father.* She sighed. *This visit will be good for mother to have us home again.* She looked at Beulah, fussing with the boy. *Beulah will be with her family, too. I know she is excited about seeing her family even though she doesn't talk about it. Maybe she will convince her brother Rufus to return with her as that is her dream and plan.*

Amelia squared her shoulders and settled her hands in her lap. She frowned as she thought of the future. She looked over at the companion who had been by her side for almost 20 years. She thought of the plans she had made during the past several winters and how exciting it was to be a part of the growing community. Now she was ready to put that all in her past. The memories came crowding in on her as the horses galloped down the dusty road north.

The first winter they boarded at the Fiske boarding house, and it suited everyone as answers to their prayers. Amelia worked for Dr. Rodney in his established clinic. Beulah did housework and cooking for Mrs. Fiske, and Sarah Marie taught school to the Fiske children, plus several of the neighbor children, holding classes in the Fiske dining room. Sarah Marie had a book case built, and a cupboard stood in the corner, its doors hiding the necessary slates, chalk, scissors, and other supplies.

After Amelia gave birth to Joseph, it was apparent to everyone that a suitable dwelling was necessary and, as luck would have it, a businessman and his family decided to sell their sturdy, four bedroom log home and return to Ohio. His wife's health was failing, and it was obvious he wanted to be near other family members to help him with his situation. Amelia was able to meet the purchase price, including furniture, for $2,500.00. Beulah, Amelia, Sarah

Marie and Joseph moved into the space the same day after the first owners moved out. Sarah Marie's cowboy friend, Jack Frey, loaded their meager belongings into his wagon and the Fiske children lined the fence, waving handkerchiefs as they watched their teacher drive away.

Beulah had a full time job caring for Amelia and her newborn son. She also continued to help out at the clinic, cleaning and doing light filing on busy days. Beulah's dream of opening her own school for colored children was put aside, but not forgotten.

Beulah planned to open a private school in the log house. Sarah Marie had moved into a rental house for the summer and coming winter with her cowboy and sweet little Helen, now a little over a year old.

Dr. Rodney spent most of his day in the mining camps, but he was talking about slowing down, cutting back on patients, semi-retiring. Also, he had mentioned that he was hiring his nephew, a recent graduate medical student. It seems the young man had a desire to travel west and, all-in-all, Amelia was happy with the news. This doctor had graduated from Harvard Medical School, the same school her father had received his doctor's degree.

When Amelia told Dr. Rodney she might not be back in the fall, he accepted the news, but with much sadness. "Please don't make that decision right now. You feel things out first. If you find opposition to your being a doctor, you skedaddle yourself right back here. There is room for all of us."

Amelia thanked him for his offer and told him she would do as he suggested. She felt in her heart she was doing the right thing for herself as well as for the future of her son. *Martin would want his son to go to Harvard like he did.* Amelia did not say this out loud, keeping her thoughts to herself. She and Dr. Rodney parted with a handshake.

The future looked bright for the town that still depended on the gold mines. Tents were slowly being replaced with wooden structures. Men created businesses. Women ran cafés, laundry houses, and boarding houses, sewed and created hats.

Amelia often drove her horse and buggy out to the North Hill where she could look down into the Prickly Pear Valley floor just as she had done upon arrival, in what now seemed like a very long time ago. It was almost like a dream to try and remember what it had looked like from that distance away, with northern winds blowing.

Now, a town of several thousand people greeted the rising sun each day to make a better life for families by hard work in the mines, timbering, growing huge gardens for food supplies, ranches and businesses. Even the telegraph had reached this remote outpost of a community. Soon the railroad would bring more and more people into the area. Churches and schools, and maybe even a library, would soon stake claim to a piece of the ground.

Mutchnik Mercantile was hard pressed to keep supplies on hand as wagon trains arrived daily in the spring and summer filled with hopeful families. Lumber was being hauled in from woods more than fifty miles distant. The noise from saws and hammers continued to be heard into the twilight hours, replacing canvas tents that dominated the poorly laid out streets. A church steeple pierced the blue sky. It was used by all denominations, taking different hours for Sunday services.

Amelia was jostled back to the present as the iron rims on the wheels of the stagecoach dug ruts even deeper into the dusty path to Fort Benton.

Jake, the driver, had made this run hundreds of times. He kept his eyes on the hillsides and knew where to look for Indians who might try to stop them.

He also worried about being robbed. Stagecoaches were vulnerable to such actions by unscrupulous men and even some notorious women. Stealing money from the men and jewelry from the women was an easy way to make a living.

Fortunately, his stage had a reputation for being well guarded. The fellow riding shotgun up on top was tough. He'd shoot off a blast when he merely suspected danger, and many a ride had turned into a wild adventure over the past few years. It made him nervous when young children were on board.

The vigilantes out of Virginia City, Montana Territory spoke for the law in these parts. He had himself, encountered a need for a payoff on a couple of occasions in the past, and kept it to himself. He suspected some of the robbers were part of the Vigilantes but he never made an issue of it when he filed papers reporting any stoppages. The Wells Fargo Stage Company's head office in San Francisco, never questioned him further, which seemed to satisfy everyone. As long as his route was kept open and safe . . . that was all he needed to know about.

Two men passengers rode along without comment and Amelia did her best to keep her son from irritating them with idle chatter or by squirming about in the coach. *I wonder if they will stop in Fort Benton, or if we will see them on the river, having business in the east just as we do.*

One of the men preferred to chomp on an unlit cigar, staring out the window. He was corpulent and the sweat beaded on his forehead. Occasionally the man would swipe it with a handkerchief. His tan tweed wool coat was a tad tight fitting. A gold watch, fob and chain, stretched across the front of the jacket. He looked like a toad squished into his corner of the bench. Amelia reasoned he was a business man, maybe an agent who took newcomers to find their deeded government lands to homestead in the territory.

The other man, a cowboy, wearing a Stetson hat that added inches to his height, looked tall with a slim build. His attire was western, consisting of a leather jacket with fringe on the sleeves, a bolo tie around his neck that sported a huge chunk of turquoise, and grey-striped wool pants. He crossed his upraised legs that sprawled on the side of the bench Amelia sat upon. His cowboy boots were well worn. She couldn't help but wonder just how comfortable those boots with raised heels really were.

He smiled at her a few times and they made casual conversation but neither had much interest in what was being said. He eventually pulled his brimmed hat down over his eyes and pretended to sleep.

Amelia watched him. *Maybe he is one of those men who has business in Chicago to make plans to sell a herd of beef at the slaughter houses,* Amelia thought. *I have heard rumors about a train being built to travel from Helena to the Deer Lodge Valley that will connect with back east tracks.*

Just then Joseph pulled back the window curtain and to his surprise, he saw a small herd of deer on the hillside. A doe stood guard while the others grazed on the fresh green grasses just up after a long, hard Montana winter. It was the "merry month of May" and Amelia felt it the best time for travels with a small child. It would be warm enough but not hot, and it would be summer in Virginia when they arrived after 45 days of weary river boat travel.

Beulah leaned over Joseph to look out the window. "Halleluiah. We is almost to Fort Benton, Miss Amelia." She clapped her hands, startling the heavy-set man. He shifted his weight toward the opposite window wanting to see what Beulah was so excited about.

"Hhrrummp! Yes. Fort Benton. At last." He pulled out his watch and studied the dial. "We are making good time today, but I am ready to find me a chair that rocks back and forth in a place that serves a good cup of tea."

He can speak, thought Amelia and she smiled holding her handkerchief over her face to hide it from the man.

The stagecoach driver deposited passengers, luggage and a mail sack onto the covered porch of the Cosmopolitan Hotel. Twilight had descended and the horses and coach were silhouetted in shadows. Joseph waved and Jake saluted him back. He shouted down to the group huddled on the porch.

"Good-day to you folks. I'm on my way to enjoy a good beer." His six horses were also anxious to reach their stable where a good brush down, water and oats were awaiting them. With a snap of the reins, the horses pulled the wagon away from the hotel and left in its stead a cloud of yellow dust.

"Come along, son. Let's check on our reservations for tonight." Amelia reached for her valise. Beulah grabbed two of the bags, then handed the smaller one to Joseph. He tugged and pulled but made it inside the hotel lobby only to drop it and stare.

"Mama, look!" It was as if he were frozen to the spot. "Look!" He pointed to the wall where taxidermy animals sat on ledges, the mountain lion ready to pounce down, and the elk seeming to come right through the wall, his rack of horns stretching easily six feet across. A cowboy hat had been tossed there some time ago, and dust had accumulated on the brim.

Amelia gave her son a push on his shoulders, moving him into the lobby where the desk clerk smiled at the three of them.

"We have reservations. Dr. A. Martin, party of three." She noticed the open dining room. "We will want meals here, also."

"Yes, Ma'am. That is all arranged. We have a room ready for you." He struck a bell on the counter and a young boy came to take the luggage. He took Amelia's bag, and Joseph's bag, but he did not pick up Beulah's. She pretended not to notice the slight as she reached for her own valise. With head held high she followed last in the parade of bodies that moved up the wooden flight of stairs to the rooms above.

Their one shared large trunk would be stored against the lobby wall to be hauled away later this evening to the river depot dock. Someone would see that it was deposited in their cabin on the boat, a service arranged by the hotel and the riverboat owners.

Beulah glanced out the small glass panes passing for a window. She and Amelia would sleep in separate cots covered with handmade patched quilts. Joseph would sleep with a pillow and blanket on the rag rug on the floor.

It will be fun to walk along the wooden sidewalks to see if the town has growed up much since we were here six years ago. But first, I want a warsh cloth to get the grime off my face, then a cup of hot tea and maybe one of those chocolate chip cookies I saw on a plate by the dining room reception desk. Beulah's shoulders slumped as weariness moved into her limbs.

Stagecoach to Fort Benton

~19~

Homestead Papers Arrive

The brisk walk to the mercantile invigorated Sarah Marie. Every day she checked for a letter for her husband. Not just any letter, but a government letter from the United States Land Department. Her friend, Josie, acted as the official postmistress.

Many months had passed since Jack had filled out the official papers applying for a homestead north of Helena. The wait seemed to take forever and it was unbearable. The Frey family had grown over the past three years and it now included two toddlers, Helen and Celine. The small house that they continued to rent in Helena on Second Street bulged at the edges. If Jack was to get in his own crop he had to be doing so within this coming month.

Josie, the post mistress, stood behind the long table that supported the mail boxes. The 4 x 6 boxes were lined up side-by-side and each had a number painted on the small glass door. A cubby-hole sized box held long envelopes and newspapers.

"Good morning, Sarah Marie. Would you know I have mail for you today?"

Josie reached into the mail box and pulled out two letters and handed them to the smiling woman.

"It's here! At last!" Sarah Marie kissed the envelope addressed to Mr. John Frey, Helena, Montana.

"Open it." Josie was as excited as Sarah Marie. "Hurry!"

Sarah Marie turned the envelope over in her hand and started to rip the flap, but she stopped. "I can't do this without Mr. Frey with me. It's addressed to him, not to me." Sarah Marie sighed. "I'll just have to wait until he comes home for dinner tonight."

Josie frowned. "You *are* his wife. Go ahead, open it."

Sarah Marie held her ground. She tucked the envelope into her reticule and turned to leave the store. "I'll let you know what it says very soon." She waved a hasty goodbye.

As she walked along the boardwalk, thankful for such a lovely late spring day with no wind, she thought about Josie and how connected she was to the community in such a short few years. Being the post mistress was a very important position. At first, Josie just took on the task as there was no official post office, but as time passed, Josie applied for the job and a post office was established in the Mutchnik building. Everyone who passed through the area could stop and check for mail. Josie held on to mail if it was addressed to a name she recognized. Most often, a drifter would claim the mail, grateful to Josie for her patience.

Sarah Marie thought about Josie's marriage to Frank Hicks. The wedding took place the same fall that she and Jack married. Josie had been married to Jeremiah Hicks, a younger brother to Frank. When she became with child, she decided to name the baby "Frankie" in honor of Jeremiah's older brother who had supplied them with money when they left for the western frontier.

Jeremiah and Mr. Mutchnik had gone up river on the Missouri River. Their plan was to set up a mercantile business and have Josie and the baby, and Mrs. Mutchnik follow them in the autumn months. Mrs. Mutchnik, Josie and Frankie joined Jeremiah in Helena after the baby was born in St. Louis.

The riverboats cut the travel time, but it was dangerous. More than half of the boats that left St. Louis, Missouri sank in the river. People drowned, along with the loss of the supplies. Jeremiah did not want Josie to be in the family way and take the risks of river travel. By the time Josie was ready to travel, the water level was lower and not as turbulent as during the spring snow run off.

They were all reunited in Fort Benton, Montana Territory that fall. They were busy building a life together.

Then tragedy struck. Jeremiah was run over by a team of horses gone wild. They were pulling a heavy wagon loaded with mine supplies, and he died from his injuries. For several years afterwards Josie and little Frankie lived with the Mutchniks, worked in their store, and saw to creating a post office.

Frank Hicks, the older brother in Virginia, sold the farm and eventually came out west. He visited Josie and little Frankie, and within a very short time, they married. Frank worked in the mercantile business assisting Mr. Mutchnik who was beginning to feel his arthritic bones, especially during the long, cold winter months. Frank's dream was to homestead north of Helena. After all, he was a born farmer and that is what he wanted to do. Frank's application for a homestead was holding him hostage.

Sarah Marie walked along the wooden street path. Now I understand her interest in my letter from the government about the homestead tract we applied for. They are probably waiting to hear from them just like we were. A smile spread across Sarah Marie's face. *I hope they hear soon.*

Back home, Sarah Marie lost count of how many times she picked up the letter. Each time, however, she set it back onto the table top, waiting for the proper time to open it with her husband. She had a beef stew simmering on the back circle on the top of the wood stove. Hot rolls were ready to be pulled from the oven. The two daughters were already fed and in bed. Darkness was taking over the spring day.

"Wouldn't you know tonight he is late for supper?" She talked out loud to the golden haired dog that lay on the rag rug by the side of the stove. Nikki perked up her ears and walked over to Sarah Marie.

"What are you doing coming into the front room? You know you are not to be in here." Nikki barked and danced around Sarah Marie's feet until she gave in. "You rascal. Come on. Let's both go into the kitchen and have something good cooking on that wood stove. I'm going to light a candle when we eat dinner and then show Mr. Frey the letter."

Nikki followed her into the kitchen, twirled around three times and dropped to the rug, resting her head on her crossed front paws.

Ten more minutes passed when the door banged open and Jack Frey hurried into the kitchen. "It's going to rain tonight. Isn't that wonderful news? We really need the moisture on our crops that are showing some green in the earth." He grabbed Sarah Marie around the waist and did a little jig with her. "What's for dinner? It sure does smell great in here. I caught a good whiff of it when I put brushed down Prunes in the barn." He wrinkled his nose. "My favorite hot rolls. What's going on?" He looked around the kitchen and saw the candle. "Is it our anniversary or something?"

"Go wash up. We'll eat as soon as you are rid of that horrible jacket you insist on wearing all the time. Wash behind your ears, too." He laughed at his wife's comments, but he hung the jacket on the special peg just outside the kitchen in the wash room. A bucket of lukewarm water waited for him to splash on to his face and hands.

Sarah Marie lit the candle in the middle of the table, put out two bowls, plates, silverware and coffee mugs. She leaned the letter addressed to Mr. John Frey against the handmade tallow candle. She pulled out two chairs, and went to the stove to remove the lid from the cast iron pot filled with the beef stew, vegetables and gravy. She ladled the mixture into the bowls. She lifted the coffeepot with her aproned hand and filled the two cups. Next, she brought heavy thick cream from the small icebox and poured a dollop into each cup.

"My dear, eat up. Did you have an extra-long day at the ranch?"

"The calving has started in full force now, and I might have to stay out some nights doing some riding on the herd. My boss doesn't like early calving because of the cold and snow and unpredictable weather, and I think he is right to wait until late spring. We have smaller calves in the fall, but he holds over quite a bunch of those calves that first winter anyway. I guess it all balances out," he sighed.

"The rain is going to be a blessing to everyone . . . as long as it doesn't turn cold during the night and chill out the calves we have already."

He talked short sentences in between bites of stew meat. "These rolls sure do sop up the gravy just right." He took a big chunk of the sour dough roll, scooping up the remaining gravy in the bottom of his bowl. He took a sip of coffee.

"Did you bring home the mail and a paper today?"

Sarah Marie, not able to stand it any longer, pointed to the letter on the table.

"Will you please open your mail? I can't wait another minute."

Jack looked at the letter, then at her. He read the return address in the left hand corner, just as she had done in the post office.

"Here, you open it."

"No. It's yours to open, but hurry, will you please? I've been waiting all afternoon for this." She put her arms around his neck and peeked over his shoulder.

"Now . . . . This very minute . . . . You open that letter."

"I need a knife to slit the edge."

Sarah Marie ran to the drawer, removed a sharp paring knife and handed it to Jack. "Now. Just *do* it."

Both Sarah Marie and Jack were holding their breath. Jack swiftly removed the several sheets of paper, and perused the front cover with one quick glance.

"Whoopee!"

He held the paper up to Sarah Marie who looked at him with questioning eyes.

"Do we have a homestead? We really do? Where? Did they send a map with directions? What do we do now? Jack, will we be able to move right soon?" She paced the kitchen floor. "We have so much to do, and I don't know where to even begin."

The two girls, rubbing sleep from their eyes, came out of their bedroom.

"Mommy, what is all the noise about? Are you all right?" asked Helen, the oldest.

"Yes, of course, my darling little girls. Mommy is just very, very happy." She pulled the two children into the folds of her skirt and stroked back their hair that was peeking out from beneath their night caps.

We are going to build a fine house one day soon. We'll have our own garden and chickens and cows and Daddy will have his own horses to break. He can raise a pig if he wants to." Sarah Marie was so excited she couldn't stop babbling.

"Come, sit at the table and I will warm up some milk for you two so you can go back to sleep. Daddy was late getting his supper tonight and I am sorry we woke you, but this is very good news. We've been waiting for a long time for this letter. We needed to get this final notice about land for us to build our life on." She smiled as she worked in the kitchen and the girls continued to look confused about the whole conversation.

The older girl leaned out of her chair and whispered to her little sister. "I'll take care of you. Don't worry. Mommy is happy." She frowned. "Whatever happens don't you worry. You and I . . . we'll stay together."

Sarah Marie set the cups of warm milk in front of the girls. "It seems all mixed up right now, children, but we will have a little ranch all to ourselves. We will build up a fine cattle herd like the one Daddy works on now." She picked up the papers on the table top and walked out of the kitchen, wanting to be alone to read every line and savor every detail that would change their lives from this day forward.

North to the Sleeping Giant

~20~

Moving to the Homestead

A spring sky full of sunshine and promise greeted the Frey family on the designated moving day. The official papers, stamped and recorded in the Federal Land Department in Washington, D.C., were in a metal letter box, placed inside a small trunk.

"The fees are all paid in full. The land is a good location and there is a spring in the field for the animals." Jack gave Sarah Marie a hug. "First thing we'll have to do is build us a house, but not before we walk off the corners and put a stack of rocks at each corner. We have to know just where to build the fence, too."

Jack's mind was swirling, full of anticipation for the work to be done during the long hours of summer sunshine.

"One good thing about Montana's summer, Sarah Marie . . . we'll have daylight until ten most every night. And, we can sleep in that tent all year if we have to." Jack pointed to the huge mound of canvas that took up most of the wagon bed. Some stove pipe, a black pot—bellied stove, and a rather large wood cook stove took up the rest of the space.

"Sure was nice of our friends to come around for moving day." Jack waved to a driver in an approaching wagon. "We will have quite a bonfire in the Wolf Creek Canyon tonight. Everyone is bringing food to share, too." Jack laughed out loud.

"It's really happening, dear wife. We are on our way."

Sarah Marie had been unusually quiet the morning of departure. The move meant isolation for her and the girls. Their nearest neighbor would be at least one section away and the homestead was open land, constant wind, and no wooded area nearby.

"I heard today that another section of land was just released. You will have neighbors and a woman friend before long, Sarah Marie. The children will have playmates soon enough, and you can be the neighborhood school teacher." As he watched his wife frown, Jack paused.

"I've got to ramrod this outfit, so you say your goodbyes and let's be on our way." Jack mounted his favorite horse, Prunes, and went in search of the wagon drivers who were gathering at the far end of the street, waiting to make a caravan headed north, some 60 miles distant from Helena. The dry-land farm was located between Augusta, and Wolf Creek, Montana.

Ladies and their children stood in a row, waiting to say goodbye to Sarah Marie and the girls. Not only were they losing their friends but their schoolmarm as well. Each lady handed a wrapped package to Sarah Marie as they gave each other hugs or shook hands. The packages contained bread, sweet rolls, coffee beans, sugar, salt, flour, potatoes and carrots and onions from their root cellar, seeds for a new garden, dried fruit, hollyhock roots, and nasturtium seeds. The lilac bushes had been dug up once again to be transplanted on the homestead. A few apple trees were also included, to be transplanted near the house, in hopes that they would take hold, providing shade and food for the Frey children.

The household had been dismantled and stored in the wagons for several days. Now the hour for departure was near. With both trepidation and excitement, Sarah Marie picked up the reins of the horses on the lead wagon. She made sure her children were secure on top of a mound of bedding before shouting, "Wagons Ho."

When she drove past the mercantile, she saw Josie standing alongside Mrs. Mutchnik who was in her fancy wheelchair. Little Frankie stood on the other side of her. He waved and shouted as the wagons went past, like he was watching a parade.

"We'll be together in the fall," shouted Josie. Then she broke from the porch group and ran out into the road. She trotted alongside the wagon and yelled at Sarah Marie. "Don't forget that we are applying for a homestead near Wolf Creek, and I'll be the post mistress there." Now out of breath, Josie stopped. She blew a kiss to the girls and stepped back to the side of the road.

One final wave and the wagon train moved into the Prickly Pear Valley. The two—day exodus would require a night camp in the canyon, and early breakfast for at least ten men. Sarah Marie had plans for their meals, and would have to rough it. The drivers would need food to make their return trip.

"Mr. Frey is going to have to set up that wood stove out on the grass. Maybe he'll have a canvas sail he can put up to keep the fire from blowing out. I've got to be able to bake biscuits and make gravy."

She turned to look at the children. They had both smuggled cats and their dog, Nikki, on board thinking no one had noticed. *This is what you wanted, woman. Now, make the best of it. I will just pray us safe.*

The wagon train had reached a steady pace, and when they neared the North Hill (or Rattlesnake Hill, as the locals called it), Sarah Marie looked back toward Helena.

She had not been up this way for many years and the sight was a surprise. She saw hundreds of tall trees, some lingering snow banks along the gullies, houses and buildings along the main street. A real town spread out over several miles attesting to its years of growth. *My goodness! When I first looked down into that valley there was nothing but sage, the wind and those splendid Rocky Mountains off in the distance. It still amazes me when I think about how brave we thought we were, moving out here, Amelia, Beulah and myself.*

"Look, girls . . . see Helena behind you?" Sarah Marie hoped they would remember this sight forever, just as she knew she would never forget.

Girls in front of tent home

*Twenty-five
years later*

~21~

Post office in Wolf Creek

A letter, wafting the aroma of rose water on the envelope, waited for Sarah Marie at the Wolf Creek Post Office. It was from Amelia, and Josie was anxious to hear Sarah Marie read it out loud to her. This had become a regular routine for the two young women as the years passed by, since Amelia had moved to her home town in Virginia rather than returning, after a few months' vacation, with her mother as originally planned.

Josie stood by the lace curtained window facing the roadway. *Sarah Marie usually comes to town on Tuesday afternoons for supplies. The girls love it when they can accompany their mother. It must be quite isolated out there on that homestead, especially during the winter. Brrr! How I wish Sarah Marie would come flying through that door just about now.*

The three bells over the door rang out announcing someone was coming into the post office section of the general store. Mr. Mutchnik had set them up in merchandise. Josie spent her time in the store, while

Frank and Frankie, now a grown man and a good farmer, worked the homestead land. The arrangement between step-father and son had worked out well, and Josie was a happy woman.

Josie and Frank, soon after their marriage, procreated a baby girl, named Violet Matilda. She had grown into a sweet little child, smart, pretty and full of energy. She was a very good student, and loved to read books. Josie tried not to spoil her, but it was such a delight to have a girl. *My goodness! What a difference it is to have a boy baby and then a girl baby. Violet is a bit precocious.*

The bells jangled again.

"Hello. Anybody here?" Sarah Marie stood at the door, swinging it back and forth.

Josie immediately broke into a smile. "I hoped you'd be coming through that door today. You have a letter from Amelia. I am dying to have you read it to me."

Sarah Marie took the envelope with the familiar handwriting and kissed the ink.

"I had a hunch . . . and Mr. Frey needs some supplies, too. If you don't have them in stock, I am to order everything on this list." She handed it to Josie. The list included various household items and some tools, all necessary on the homestead.

"I'll round up your requests, all in good time, yes, in good time. But read me the letter, please?" Josie folded her hands together as if in prayer.

Sarah Marie pulled off her cloak and bonnet. Farm women never left home summer or winter without proper covering from the sun. They were very protective of their white skin and, in their vanity, tried to diminish wrinkles and crow's feet around their eyes. Sarah Marie had made her Prairie Madonna bonnet out of a bright blue paisley print. She stiffened the brim by sewing in heavy cut-to-fit cardboard to shade her eyes. This insert was removed before washing the bonnet.

As was Sarah Marie's habit, she carefully lifted the envelope flap and began to read, slowly and out loud at first. But her eyes began to scan the pages faster than she could speak the words. "Amelia is coming for a visit. She is bringing Mother, Beulah and Joseph." Sarah Marie twirled around and she handed the letter to Josie. "Here, you can read it yourself."

~22~

Amelia Writes to Sarah Marie

Dear Sarah Marie and husband Jack,

Are you sitting down to read this letter? I have exciting news.

Mother, Joseph Beulah and of course, me, are planning to come west by train for a lengthy visit. We will arrive on the first day of July at the ungodly hour of nine o'clock in the evening. The train is much faster than coming up river like we did, remember?

So many years have separated us and Mother wants to see her "baby girl" one more time before she reaches the age where she cannot travel because of declining health. We never should have allowed so much passage of time. However, we have all lived fulfilling lives where God planted us, haven't we?

Your letters have kept the family together, my dear little sister. Whenever one arrived I gathered the family into the parlor and read your words out loud. Joseph still clings to the image of Auntie Sarah Marie, so both of you will be surprised when you finally meet once again. He is no longer a little five-year-old boy, but a handsome young man, graduated from Harvard Medical School, following in his mother's tradition of a Roberts physician in our village. Remember, our grandfather started it, then our father, then I, and I can't forget Joseph's father, James . . . and now Joseph. I am very proud of him.

You won't recognize me. I am gray and wrinkled. Returning home was a good choice for me. Joseph is happy. I am content living in the family home. Beulah still oversees everything and everyone.

I have a request to make of you. Would you please find us rooms for at least 60 days? Perhaps a house for rent, or rooms in a hotel that also caters meals? We will need a large buggy and horse team to get us around.

I realize you and Jack will be far too busy to entertain us for the summer months . . . or maybe longer depending on the weather.

We won't even recognize the town we helped to create, since it is grown into a fine city, what with the capitol of the State of Montana hosting the seat of political government.

I want to show Joseph the shack where he was born, where we lived at the Fiske Boarding House, the clinic, everything.

To finally meet your children will be an emotional happiness for all of us. Mother will be overcome by it all. Should our plans change, I'll send a telegram. Until we can once again hug each other, I pray you all stay well and be happy.

Your loving sister,
Amelia

Sarah Marie asked Josie for paper, pencil, an envelope and a stamp.

Dear Amelia,

Your letter arrived today and I can barely believe my eyes. Breathing normally is impossible. Is it true? Are you really coming for a visit? Oh, I am so happy to be able to see you after all these years and to introduce Mother to her wonderful granddaughters, and to her great-grandson . . . my grandson Jack, who is like a son to me. After Helen, our oldest died after childbirth, we naturally raised him as our own. But you know all about this.

We will meet your train; secure rooms at the Grand Central Hotel, and a buggy and team will be hired at the Payne Stables.

I will recognize you, my dear sister. Don't worry about being in our way. Summer months are the only safe time to travel. You will recognize me because I have not changed one bit. Ha, ha.

We are all still reeling financially and emotionally from the winter of 1886. Mr. Frey will be haying, with one eye on the ground and the other watching the clouds. Hail storms come up so suddenly and do much damage. Remember the hail storm we were in?

We call this land "Next Year Country," because we have to remain optimistic when nature is cruel to us. But the climate, sunshine, healthy children, my happy husband, and our homestead, all make up the good side of that coin.

Sadly, there never was enough in savings for me to take a frivolous trip on a train, or to skip out on the farm chores always waiting to be done.

I want to post this letter today while I am here in Josie's store. She loves it when you write, as I read the letter to her and she passes the information on to Frank.

We will plan to be together very soon. Joseph and Little Frankie, oops! We don't call him 'little' any more . . . Maybe the men can take a day and go fishing in the Dearborn River after working in the hay fields. I'll have plenty of work clothes for Joseph to wear.

Affectionately,
Sarah Marie

Grand Central Hotel

~23~

Joseph James Martin Returns

The tall, slender-built and handsome young man in a fashionable gray wool suit stepped from the train stairway and paused on the platform. He looked quickly into the evening shadows to the right and then to the left side of the depot. The gas lit lamp post, shining not too far away, cast a glow, enabling him to see the hands on his gold pocket watch with the spring snap lid, stamped *Made in Germany* on the reverse side. He never tired of looking at the gift from his mother upon his graduation from Harvard School of Medicine. He was proud of his achievements, following in the footsteps of his great grandfather, grandfather, father and mother, all alumnae from Harvard Medical School.

There was a commotion behind him as an elderly woman struggled with a cumbersome circular hat box. Her travel suit, of sapphire blue wool, looked exquisite on a very well-kept slender body. A matching reticule, larger than normal, swung from her left wrist.

"Joseph, please take this box from me so I can navigate these five steps gracefully."

The young man turned, grabbed the box, swung it to the platform and repeated the movement, helping the older woman, his grandmother, to reach solid ground.

"At last we are *here*." She straightened her hat decorated with a feathery plume, unaware that they were being observed by a group, probably a farm family, judging by their clothing. An older couple, four lovely young women, and a teenaged boy stood very still, waiting for directions from their father. The contrast was stark, almost cruel.

The man spoke to his family. "What are you waiting for? There stands your mother and your sister Amelia." As if on cue, the group moved as one through the station door and spilled out onto the platform. Sarah Marie ran the short distance and felt herself being wrapped up in a gentle but firm bear hug. She looked into the face of her mother and smiled.

"It has been way too long between 'hello and goodbye,' Mother. I am so happy you made this long, arduous trip to come visit me." She stepped back, still holding her mother's hands. "Wait until you meet your son-in-law. He's a real cowboy. You have four granddaughters and they all look like you."

She motioned to the girls, Jack and the boy to come forward to meet their grandmother for the very first time. Over the years there had not been any extra money for picture taking. However, the grandmother had only to gaze into their eyes to find the recognition and resemblance she had prayed she would find when she reached this destination. She was not disappointed.

Sarah Marie fell into her sister's arms and felt the beating of her heart against her calico dress.

"Amelia. Oh! Amelia. Thank God you have come back to us." She pushed her sister away from her at arm's length, and then pulled her to her again. Tears shimmered from the two women's smiling eyes as they embraced.

"I've waited for so long to see you again. You look wonderful. You look like *Mother* the last time I saw her . . . how long ago?" She turned her attention to the young man. "Joseph, how you have grown. What a fine looking man you are today. Don't be shy. Come and give your Auntie Sarah Marie a hug." Sarah Marie wiggled her fingers motioning Joseph to move to her.

Joseph swiftly did as asked. He was surprised that this farm woman was his aunt; or that he even recognized her. Perhaps what he *recognized* was the family resemblance, but he thought of it as seeing her inner strength and spirit of happiness and peace.

"Let me introduce you to your cousins." Sarah Marie walked behind the row of girls and tapped each on the shoulder as she announced their names. "Celine, Elsie, Gertrude and Nora Bea, this is your cousin, Joseph James." The girls giggled and held out their hands for Joseph to shake, one at a time. The lone teenaged boy at the end of the line stepped forward. "Hi. My name is Jack."

Meanwhile, Mr. Frey stood patiently in the background; he came forward and shook Joseph's hand. "Hello son, welcome back to your birthplace. Sarah

157

Marie has so much to show you, and to tell you about our homestead." He smiled as he looked over the tops of the heads of his family.

He reached for Sarah Marie's hand while she announced her news.

"I've made reservations for all of us to stay tonight in the Grand Central Hotel. It's on Main Street, Amelia." She turned to Beulah. "Your room will be in a separate section for servants, and breakfast will be in the kitchen." Beulah smiled and said nothing.

"Oh! Wait until you see how this town has grown. It's too late to go sight-seeing tonight, but first thing in the morning, Mr. Frey is going to take us for a town tour." She smiled brightly at her sister and her nephew.

"I wish we had thought to hire a photographer to capture this moment." She pointed to the train, huffing, steaming and vibrating the ground behind the group. "Isn't it wonderful you can arrive by the luxury of a train now? You saved many days by not coming up river."

Jack Frey watched as two muscular black men unloaded luggage, wooden crates, canvas pouches, milk cans, mail sacks, and animals in pens from the freight cars near the end of the train. He walked toward that area, turned to motion to the group to follow, and proceeded to lead a parade of happy, laughing people to claim and collect all their possessions.

Joseph held his grandmother's elbow with his right hand and carried her hat box in the other. When Mr. Frey saw the stacks of boxes he prayed it wasn't all to go to Amelia. *Where will I put all of this stuff and the humans too? I only brought one wagon.* "Oh . . . my!"

Amelia saw him frown. "Jack this isn't all mine."

She laughed the same laugh he had heard almost thirty years ago and felt an inner glow spread through his chest. It was good for the family to be able to spend the summer months together, even if it was their busiest season, with crops nearing harvest, turkeys, chickens, and a huge garden to tend to every day.

Jack brought the wagon team up closer to the freight boxcar. *Sarah Marie will fit it all in. Or, I'll take them all to the hotel and come back for the luggage. Yes, that is a better idea.*

"Amelia, can you point out what is yours, please? And then I want you all to get into the wagon. Amelia you sit in front. Joseph help her and watch that first step, it is a high one."

Joseph looked at his mother and smiled. "We are used to walking, sir, and the hotel is just down the platform a short distance. I'll accompany the ladies who want to walk."

"That's up to you then. I'll get the luggage and meet you all at the hotel."

With a snap of the reins, the team sprang into motion and lumbered on past the buildings that Amelia had never seen.

"I don't know where to rest my eyes. Everything is so different. This can't possibly be my Helena. Who are all these people and what do they do here?"

"Helena is the capitol city, sister. We won the privilege a few years back. The elected governor is Joseph K. Toole. He and his wife live in Helena in a mansion built just for the governor. You'll see all of this tomorrow."

They walked briskly along the train platform. Just then the Grand Central Hotel came into sight. Amelia gasped at the beautiful three-story building. Its lights, shining through the windows, welcomed them to step inside the hotel. Sarah Marie took charge, rang the service bell at the counter, and secured keys for the rooms.

Meanwhile, Mr. Frey had returned to collect the luggage and freight. *This is going to be good for Sarah Marie. I know it has been difficult being married to me, living on our homestead but, all in all, we've been happy I think. She never complains about it, anyway. Staying in the fancy hotel is going to be expensive. God knows, I've not been able to treat her to anything special for many years.* He drove the team and wagon close to the hotel entrance. The young man who came to assist him was strong and knew where to unload.

"Please put the items that belong to Dr. Martin together. We'll know in the morning what arrangements are to be made."

"Yes sir. This underground storage area will work just fine and is safely locked at all times."

Jack found the women chatting in their sitting room sipping tea and eating cookies. The two young men were chatting in a small bedroom area discussing the homestead. The contrast jarred him into reality. He gazed tenderly at his wife. *Sarah Marie once looked like a delicate flower with flawless, creamy white skin. Now she's wrinkled, and even though she has worn her Prairie*

Madonna bonnet for protection from the sun, her face has a leathered, tanned look.

He did not announce his presence. Watching his daughters talking and laughing gave him a happy feeling. Sarah Marie had done a superb job at raising their children, educating them with books she had brought on her initial trip out west. Over the years, Amelia had supplied her with teaching materials as well. The older girls had been hinting they would like to attend school, maybe back east, for professional training as teachers, doctors, nurses, or entering into the man's world of business.

Maybe Amelia will steal my oldest girls away from me by the end of summer. She can offer them the keys to their dreams. Jack shook his head. *Whoa, there. Settle down. Don't go getting ahead of yourself. What becomes of this visit? Only time will reveal the answer to that question.*

"There you are. Did you get the horses to the stable already?" Sarah Marie walked over to the door frame and took hold of her husband's arm. Jack noticed how shabby her best dress looked next to Amelia's travel suit. *Why, her hat alone probably cost as much as all the calico print Sarah Marie used to make pinafores for the girls. The clothes in the trunks left in the basement are probably fancy back east styles, not suited for our boardwalks and gravel streets. I hope it doesn't create a problem for the women.*

Jack stood next to Sarah Marie. "Ladies and gents, it has been a long day for all of us. Let us separate now, and plan to meet in the lobby at eight o'clock tomorrow morning."

He turned to Amelia. "If that is an appropriate time, Amelia, the hotel has a full European breakfast. Then we will get on with the Helena tour."

"Fine, Jack. We will be ready and waiting." Amelia turned to Sarah Maria and smiled. "Sister, how I have longed for us to be together again. Thank God for the completion of the railroad, even as expensive as it was to build it." She gave her sister a hug. "See you in the morning. Goodnight to everyone."

The breakfast meal was pleasant. Amelia and the desk clerk worked out plans for trunk storage and room arrangements: a room for Amelia and her mother, a room for Joseph, and a bed in the servant's quarters for Beulah, to occupy them for at least sixty days. The desk clerk also gave Amelia a receipt for the arrangements made for a buggy and horse rental.

Beulah would be allowed into the hotel since the anti-segregation bill had just passed into law. She could not be served in the dining room, however. Her meals would be served in the kitchen along with the help.

Sarah Marie planned to stay in Helena with her sister and mother. The daughters would leave the next morning with their father back to the homestead. Joseph would return Sarah Marie. The plans were made to everyone's satisfaction.

Since they did not know how much time they would spend on the homestead, the hotel manager decided Amelia could pay full price for the days they used the rooms and a storage fee for the other times when the rooms were empty. The hotel was three stories high, with the top floor for women, the middle floor for men and cowboys, and the first floor occupied by the lobby and dining room.

Nora Bea had thoughtfully made a list of buildings, parks, churches and other places of interest that were not present when Amelia doctored years ago. Helena now boasted a hospital. Dr. Rodney's clinic on top of the hill was no more. A new building stood at that address and now housed an attorney.

"Thank you, Nora. This is so thoughtful. We will also have to drive to China Town and show Joseph an abacus. Are any of the Wong's still here?" She saw her sister shake her head up and down. Amelia clapped her hands in excitement. "We'll eat an early supper at Yatson's Noodle Parlor tonight."

Main Street Helena, Montana Territory
Photo from the collection of the State of Montana
Historical Society, Helena, Montana

~24~

Tour of the town

"Look, Joseph. See that little shack sitting back off the road? Yes, that one with the school bell on the porch." Amelia pointed to the tiny wood-sided house, now the home of a bachelor miner.

Joseph looked at the house quizzically, and then turned to face his mother. "Yes, Mother. I see it, but what . . . why are *you* so excited to see it?"

"You were born in that very house, son. The Mutchnik's lived there. Mrs. Mutchnik was a patient of mine and I went to make a house call. While there you decided it was time for you to meet the world." Amelia stretched her body to the right so she could see the old house from a more direct angle. "Please stop the horses, Jack. I want to walk over to the mercantile building, too."

Joseph hopped from the wagon and helped his mother to the ground. Together, they walked to the shack, knocked on the door and received no answer. They pushed back the tall dried weeds and peeked into the front window.

"Oh . . . my!" Mrs. Mutchnik would be so stressed to see her house looking this way." Amelia frowned but continued her story. "When we first arrived in the community there were very few houses for anyone to rent. Most people lived in canvas or animal hide tents. Luckily for us we were able to take room in the Fiske house and boarded there for almost a year." She took a breath and stepped back from the window. "I've seen enough. Let's continue on our tour." She reached for her son's arm to help her back to the wagon.

"I would like to see the cemetery one day and pay respects to the Mutchniks. Who took over the mercantile business? Did Josie and Frank and little Frankie stay in Helena?"

Sarah Marie shook her head. "Well, for a while they did, and Frank ran the mercantile rather well. But they wanted to homestead near Wolf Creek and when the opportunity came up, they did move north. Josie runs the mercantile business from a store in Wolf Creek and she is the United States Postmistress. Frank and Frankie, we don't call him Little Frankie anymore, take care of the ranch and the homestead place. They own it fair and square. It's nice to have them as neighbors. Well, we call them neighbors, but there are miles of acres separating us. We do visit when I go to town." Sarah Marie paused as if thinking. "You will see them when we drive out to the ranch."

Just then the team pulled up to a huge building, obviously the beginnings of a magnificent church. The foundation and windowless walls took over a whole city block, and hundreds of men were working on setting the stones.

"I don't believe it. A cathedral, here?"

"We have many millionaires living here, Amelia. Helena is a gold miner's dream and more rich men live here than in New York City." He smiled as he brought the team to a halt.

"A newspaper reporter from the *Independent Herald* waved his Donegal tweed cap high into the air one afternoon, many years ago, when he saw some mighty important men from the community coming out of the Grand Central Hotel. He wanted to get a story from these fellows. One of the men was the Catholic bishop, Bishop Brondel." Joseph looked at his uncle with great interest.

"The reporter shouted at the bishop and the men stopped. He asked the bishop what he would do with one hundred thousand dollars." Jack laughed. "You know what that man answered?"

"No, I have no idea what he answered."

"Well, he shouted back to the reporter without hesitation. "I'd build a mighty cathedral so that all of the people could congregate under one roof." The bishop thought for a second and then he continued. "I'll never live to see it, but that is my answer to your question."

By now the women were standing on the ground staring at the construction site. "Senator Thomas Walsh, Col. Thomas Cruse, Peter Larsen and some others I've forgotten, were the group of men walking with the bishop. They had just witnessed the planting of the seeds for the building to be rooted firmly into the soil of this little village of less than 7000 people." Jack Frey pointed to a sign with an artist's drawing nailed to it. "This is what it's going to look like."

The group studied the drawing and was amazed at the structure's size. A gothic design with arches, pillars, crosses and bell towers reached high into the brilliant blue Montana sky.

"It came to pass that the men agreed to put up money to get the plans drawn and construction supplies ordered. Bishop Brondel did not live to see his cathedral, but the next bishop, Bishop Carroll, did approve of the project. It's going to take years to complete it, but it is giving work to hundreds of men and is bringing newcomers into the area faster than we ever thought possible."

Jack was happy to be talking about this project as he was interested in watching it rise up out of the ground when he came to Helena on business.

"When Bishop Brondel gave his approval, he announced to the board members in a meeting, 'Gentlemen! We are building a mighty cathedral.'"

Amelia shielded her eyes from the rising sun and stared into the heavens. "What is the safety record? Have there been fatalities or injuries?"

"No ma'am. I am proud to say not one person has been injured so far. Men from all over the world are working here. Different languages are heard on Main Street every day.

Men volunteer work time and many families have promised to tithe twenty-five cents a week for three years. The stained glass windows will be the next big push, and the patterns are being drawn now by a glass maker from Germany by the name of O. F. Zettler. It

is going to take probably fifteen years or more to get them all in place. The Easty Pipe Organ Company from Vermont is contracted to put in 3,500 pipes in the choir lofts."

Sarah Marie cut in. "Just to get the building to this point has taken seven years." Excitement shone in her eyes and her voice rose up a pitch. "Marble from the same quarry that Michelangelo sculpted his famous statues will be in this church. Isn't that amazing? The directors tell us that green marble from Ireland is ordered to arrive any day now, too."

Amelia remained very still and quiet. "Who donated the money?"

"The most generous of all was Thomas Cruse. He came from Ireland about the same time we came west, and he mined north of here at Marysville. He named that town after his friend who boarded him up there when he was broke. They called him "Crazy Tommy" for quite a few years. He never learned to read or write, but he opened a bank, married the senator's daughter, and is a very wealthy millionaire. We'll drive past his mansion." Sarah Marie looked at her husband. He snapped the reins and the horses picked up speed.

Jack took back the conversation. "There will be two towering bell houses holding fifteen bells. Two of them will weigh over 3,500 pounds and will swing. The others will have a striker that will ring out when the Caroler pulls the long ropes from inside the choir loft. He will call the people to Mass, alert us if there are emergencies in the mines, and toll the bells at funerals."

As an after-thought Jack continued, "In the twelfth century, gothic churches rang the bells believing the bell had the power to scare away evil. If people got inside they were safe from the dangers of the world." Jack motioned for them to all get back into the wagon box. "We are not going to see everything before dark, if we don't keep moving." Everyone laughed as they returned to the wagon and heard the teams of horses nickering to each other across the lot.

Jack Frey continued south to Rodney Street. "Do you remember where you are now, Amelia? I know it has changed a bit over the years, but the Fiske house still stands. The trees and lilac bushes are taller and I think they might have added a porch in the past year or so. Fiske's still live there, too, but Elizabeth has moved to California. She didn't like the cold winters as she got older." He chuckled at his own joke. *I don't care much for the Montana winters either.*

"We better stop by the stables and make sure the buggy and horse is available for your use." Jack was surprised when Amelia about jumped off the seat when an explosion rocked the ground.

"Are they still hard rock mining around here?" She looked across the gulch at the mine entrance and was immediately flooded with a painful memory. In her mind's eye she saw smoke coming from that hole, and remembered the chaos as men were injured. She saw her beloved Jeremiah stretched on a plank being carried in to her clinic on Rodney Street. Amelia felt Joseph looking at her and she turned her head away.

Amelia shuddered as if a cold wind had blown across her dress. "Yes, let's take care of the necessary business. Then we'll find a nice café for a noon meal, my treat."

"We'll find us a fun place, Auntie Amelia," shouted the Frey girls in unison. "We are hungry and thirsty, too." Nora Bea pretended to faint and fell onto her sister Gertrude's lap, who pushed her to the wagon floor.

Photo from the collection of the State of Montana
Historical Society, Helena, Montana

Payne Hotel

Fiske House

Pioneer Cabin

Guardian of the Gulch

Cathedral of St. Helena

Governor's Mansion

Payne Stables

~25~

Tourists

As the days sped by, the visitors enjoyed each new surprise as planned by Sarah Marie. Jack Frey, the girls and Jackie, had returned to the homestead the second day as there was work to do. A neighbor had offered to feed the dogs and milk the dairy cows, and Jack was most appreciative of his help. But, frankly, a day or two of Helena was enough for him. He preferred ranch life with its challenges over the fretful chaos of city dwellers. However, he was pleased to be able to give Sarah Marie this time to enjoy a few days vacationing with her sister. The girls were old enough to see to their chores, feeding chickens, slopping hogs, fixing meals from the canned goods in the root cellar.

Joseph handled the horses and buggy very well. He would be driving to the homestead in another week, taking Sarah Marie back to her nest.

Although Sarah Marie had faithfully written to her sister at least once a year, Amelia was overwhelmed by the population growth, businesses and houses. Actually seeing the changes made a deep impression upon her heart.

She leaned over to her sister's side of the wagon.

"We really were in on the very beginning of this mining camp, weren't we?" She laid her hand on Sarah Marie's arm. "It all seems so long ago, now, like I am being transported into my past, but forwarded into the community's future." She waved her arms in an arc. "Just look at all the trees and bushes and streets and houses, and . . . . oh, look over there. That warehouse being built . . . what do you think will be sold in there?"

Sarah Marie laughed. "That, dear sister is the Power Townsend Company. They freight goods from Fort Benton, like furniture, as well as farm implements. Mr. Mutchnik would be proud, or maybe worried about the competition, if he were alive today." The two sisters sighed.

Joseph couldn't help but laugh at the reaction from his mother every time Sarah Marie pointed out a new building. "I plan to take you to the cemetery this afternoon. Will that be agreeable to you three?"

Amelia looked at the other women, and then spoke to Joseph. "Thank you, son. The cemetery stop is very important to me." She searched the area for lilac bushes in bloom, planning to take flowers to the stones in mind.

Amelia smiled a sad smile and looked up to the majestic mountain-top sky line. "I never forgot the very first time we saw that sky line. Do you remember it?" Amelia turned to Beulah and waited for her to answer.

"Remember it? Laws, yes. I fell in love with this God-forsaken place the minute we were slowed down on the North Hill by that farm wagon. We didn't know it was full of the Mutchniks, Josie and Jeremiah Hill, and that other couple who stayed here only a few months. Remember, they left when they heard how horrible the winters were?" She shrugged. "I wonder how they fared in life? Did anybody ever hear from them again?" She paused. "Probably no one did . . . no reason to hear from them as they weren't kin to any of us."

Amelia looked at Beulah and smiled. *Beulah has been with us for so many years she thinks of us as her kin.*

"My . . . my. We left our mark on this town, Beulah, me, with my doctoring practice, and you with your volunteering to teach folks in your church to read and write. Here we are, old and gray, wrinkled and aging just like this town." Amelia looked toward the park they were nearing. "Who knows? There just might be a monument to us inside that park."

The women howled in a cacophony of noise while Joseph continued to drive the team, a puzzled expression on his face. He just couldn't understand what all these remembrances were about, and why they held such great importance to the women.

To him, this town looked just like any other town he'd been to, except Boston, of course, which was probably 10 times larger. He wasn't expected to remember Helena, as he had only been about five years of age when he and his mother, and Beulah had left by stagecoach. So far, nothing looked familiar, but maybe he'd recognize the house he lived in as a child. Sarah Marie promised to show them that after lunch.

"Joseph, pull to a stop and let the horses rest, will you please? We need to step out of this buggy and stretch ourselves, maybe find a café for some tea."

Joseph made note of a group of business houses and he saw a sign, EDDY CAFÉ, swinging in the wind. He stopped the buggy near a statue of a little black boy holding out his arm with a lantern in his hand. The other hand held a metal ring that Joseph could securely tie the reins. A tree shaded that part of the street.

He put the buckets with the long straps on them over the ears and noses of the horses. They were filled with oats for the horses to chomp on.

He watched the women as they walked in step across the busy street. *Women are amazing creatures. They can find the good in almost everything. They never have time for tears.* He hurried to catch up. Maybe he could get some sweet tea at this café. One could dream anyway.

The tinkling bell alerted Rose that she had business. She smiled at the young man who held the door open as four women entered her café. Eddy Café was one of the few in town that did not have a "NINA" sign keeping the Irish from entering. Rose was also proud of the fact that she did not have a "No Coloreds Served Here" sign in the window. The people from the south arrived in droves after the Civil War, as they had no place to go except west.

Beulah looked around the café and was pleased with the surroundings. A clean, well swept floor greeted them, as well as table tops that were not cluttered with dirty dishes from previous customers. She waited until the other ladies were seated before she allowed herself to sit on a wooden bench. Joseph pulled up a chair to sit at the end of the long table. A little bouquet of fresh wild flowers decorated the center of each table.

"May I bring you all water?"

Amelia looked up into Rose's smiling face.

"Yes, please. Water is what we need at the moment. It's warming up right smartly today." She waited for the waitress to give them menus.

"Each day we serve whatever I like to cook and I don't have menus. Today I have a wonderful potato, bacon, cheese soup that will fill you up 'til dinner time, I guarantee it."

"Fine," said Amelia. "Please bring us all your special meal."

Joseph held up his right hand to keep her for a minute longer at the table. "We would all like sweet tea, nice and cold." He smiled.

"Sweet tea . . . uum. I can bring it if you tell me how to make it." Rose was kidding with her customers, as she loved to do. When she saw the crestfallen look on the young man's face, she burst out laughing. "Of course I make sweet tea. Honey, I'm from the south of Georgia, home of sweet tea."

Everyone joined in the joke and laughed over it again when Rose brought the glasses to the table.

"Honey, its making stuff stay cold that's my biggest problem. I get ice delivered from the ice company on Main Street once a week in the winter and every day in the summer." She sighed. "Some day they will have an icebox that doesn't decide to thaw and overflow during the middle of the night when no one is here. I don't know how many mornings I open the door to a puddle of water in my kitchen. I tend to forget to empty out the catch-all tray before I turn the key in the lock and go home."

Next, Rose brought the bowls of steaming potato bacon soup. The soup was thick as gravy. The homemade hard rolls were just perfect for sopping up liquid in the bottom of the bowl.

Rose was quick on her feet when she saw Joseph searching her counter for something sweet. She had just made a fresh apple pie that morning.

"Honey. Would you like a slice of my homemade apple pie? I'll toss in a chunk of cheddar to grate over the top of the crust, if you like."

"How can I refuse?" Joseph looked at each lady seated around him. "Bring us all pie. We're celebrating today."

"Pie it is." Rose chuckled to herself as she brought the whole pie to the table with a knife and clean plates. "Have at it, folks." She returned to her counter stool to figure up the bill. "This is a good day for Eddy Café." She started to figure out the total for sweet tea, soup, pie and cheese.

Letterhead

179

Women wear their tears like elegant jewelry.
Author Unknown

~26~

Visiting the Cemetery

There were five cemeteries: Benton Avenue Cemetery; Jewish Cemetery; Resurrection Cemetery on the outskirts of town going northeast for the Catholics; Forestvale Cemetery located a few miles northwest of town for the Protestants, and the Chinese cemetery located behind Forestvale.

Their last destination, Forestvale, drew the most interest. Joseph noticed the women peering off towards the graves, shading their eyes with their hands. He knew something important was about to take place, but for the life of him, he didn't know what it would be, or why.

They looked for names on large pieces of granite tombstones and there was no hurrying the three women. They searched until all the names written on the notepaper in his mother's handwriting were accounted for. A prayer, spoken over each departed soul, brought tears to their eyes at almost every stone.

"Joseph, go slower, please. We don't want to pass up anyone." Amelia had her list of the deceased and she intended to leave a can full of lilac blooms at most of the stones. (Luckily, the hotel provided them with tin cans that had once held stewed tomatoes. There was a stockpile of them at the back side of the building.) The maintenance man at the Grand Central Hotel had cut a large stack of lilac stems taking the cuttings from bushes surrounding the hotel yard. Fortunately, the lilacs were blooming later than usual this year and, although skimpy, the leaves still looked fresh and green. He supplied an old beer barrel that he'd filled with water after lifting it into the buggy floor.

Sarah Marie's mother opted to stay at the hotel as it had already been a long day with sightseeing, listening to the siblings talking about their lives. She intended to nap awhile and be rested for a lovely dinner later that evening.

"Joseph . . . stop . . . we will walk from here."

Joseph pulled the team to a halt under a huge cottonwood tree and the ladies climbed out without his help. He stayed back by the buggy, not wanting to interfere unless and until he was called upon to do so.

"Look, Beulah. Here lie the Mutchniks, side by side in death just as they always were in life." Amelia took hold of Beulah's offered arm and knelt down on the ground, automatically pulling weeds before setting down the flowers.

Sarah Marie wandered a slight distance to the west of the others, and then abruptly stopped.

"I just found the twins that Mrs. Fiske lost in that horrible flu epidemic ten years ago." Sarah Marie frowned. "She almost didn't make it through that time, Amelia. In fact, she and Mr. Fiske moved to California. They left their other children here tended by family members, as they were older and did not want to leave." She shook her head. "Eventually, though, they all left here and attended schools in the East, married and I don't think any of them ever did come back to Helena. A cousin lives in the house now."

Amelia walked between the stones, nodding recognition at the names of people who had been her patients so many years ago. "These pioneers were mighty tough stock. I remember some of their ailments. Now we have medications that would help prolong their lives." She took a breath. "Mostly, the accidents were the hardest for me."

The stone cutters from years past were artists who liked to design attention—drawing monuments to show respect for the lives lived. Amelia walked up to one such stone.

"Just look at this stone. It is for a child who passed twenty years ago. This is so poignant. The rocking chair, chiseled with the baby blanket draped over the edge of the chair arm . . . Oh! See the tiny carved shoes and a rattle cut out on the base, too." She let her hand drift to touch the hard rock. "I'm leaving flowers here." The lilacs added a bit of color to the otherwise drab barren earth. Amelia glanced at the information at the base of the chair. "This child died on December 25, 1883."

Beulah dropped to the ground. She had found the final resting place of her friend Moses. She began singing an old Negro spiritual. Amelia, Sarah Marie and Joseph listened, as her voice grew in volume and confidence.

"Go Down Moses, Down to Jerusalem . . ."

Beulah was wrapped in the memory of the shooting death of her courting man. Beulah's behavior startled Joseph. He had never known about Beulah having a beau. He left the horses and ran to her side.

"Beulah let me help you stand up." He extended out his arm and she gratefully accepted. A smile crossed her otherwise pained expression. It was clear she still held feelings for this man gone from her life in an instant.

"Will you tell me about Moses?"

Beulah stared off toward the north. "He was shot in the back over that precious gold the men search for in secret gulches."

Beulah then looked to her feet. "He helped your Mama, Sarah Marie and me move in to the Fiske Boarding House, and we both knew right away we was to be good friends."

Joseph waited to hear more, but Beulah moved on down the row of gravesites.

"This land surely needs tendin'. I doubt it gets water 'cept what the good Lord drops down. Umhum . . . sure can use some rain here, Lord."

Suddenly, Sarah Marie stopped and turned to the group. "Here is where my Helen was put to rest." No one spoke. Amelia went to stand next to her sister.

"Helen insisted she didn't need to be in the hospital in Great Falls when it came time for her to deliver her boy,

Jackie." She sighed. "But she should have been. Three other ladies died at that same clinic she went to that same week. An investigation was held. All the trouble came from a nurse who carried bacteria in her unwashed hair."

Amelia did not know this part of the story. "I am so sorry I was not here for you, little sister. You and Jack have struggled for so long on your homestead." Amelia just shook her head slowly and remained quiet. What could she say? Nothing. What could she do? Nothing. Just stand here and acknowledge her niece, a precious first born named Helen, who died in a tragic way.

"A huge cloud passed overhead blocking the sun for a few minutes, providing the group with much needed shade and the accompanying wind that cooled their skin.

"Helen was only 23 years old. She was married to E.S., a salesman who moved around a lot, and he couldn't take care of Jackie. So, Jack and I took him and raised him as our son. He and Jack have a wonderful relationship and we do not look upon him as a grandson. The girls think he is their brother, especially Gertrude and Nora Bee." As if an afterthought, Sarah Marie said, "E.S. comes and visits whenever he wants. Jack knows who is father is, but he prefers to live on the ranch with us."

Joseph was shocked at all he had to comprehend in this short visit to the cemetery. "You women are absolutely remarkable." He turned to his mother. "I had no idea what living out west was like for all of you." He paused, and then looked at his Auntie Sarah Marie. "It is going to be interesting to compare how you live on your ranch, and with how we live in Virginia."

Beulah snorted. "Boy, you have no idea." A belly laugh erupted from her. "I would do it all over again if the good Lord gave me the chance." She pulled on the strings that held her slat-bonnet in place.

They passed by a manmade lake in the center of Forestvale Cemetery. "This lake looks kind of like a cemetery in Brooklyn."

Joseph heard a Meadowlark sing and he turned toward the sound, where another stone caught his attention.

He recognized the Hicks name on the main headstone and read in bold script, *JEREMIAH JAMES HICKS*. He caught up with his mother and took her elbow to guide her to the Hicks Family plot.

"Mother, just look at all the stones with Hicks chiseled on them. Do you think they could be related to the Hicks family from that farm down the road not too far away from our house?"

Amelia saw the puzzled look on her son's face. She quickly set down her last can of lilacs and blinked back tears. *This is no time for tears. I decided before Joseph was born that I would not ever reveal to him my past love . . . the love I still feel for Jeremiah. Joseph's father's story is all he needs to know. Joseph has never questioned his middle name, James.*

Amelia moved quickly to the far end of the fenced-in area. She needed a private moment to collect her thoughts and she kept her back to the rest of the group.

"Miss Amelia? Are you all right?" Beulah hurried to her side, sympathy showing in her tear-filled eyes.

"I'm fine, Beulah. I just need a moment to say a silent prayer. My grief is so tightly wrapped around my heart, even today." She smiled at her friend. "It never stops hurting, don't we both know?" Amelia discreetly dabbed a handkerchief at her eyes and wet cheeks.

She called out to the others.

"Look over the fence. You will see stones written in Chinese. This whole section is dedicated to their race."

Joseph decided it was time to return to the hotel. The women looked wretched and thirsty. He needed a drink of something stronger than water. He turned on his heels and with a backhanded wave shouted, "Stay here, ladies, enjoy the shade from those huge cottonwood trees. I'll fetch the horses and buggy".

Amelia watched her handsome son walk away from her, and at that moment her heart leaped in her chest.

No . . . no . . . no! Dear God, what have I done by bringing him out west? Please, Joseph, please . . . don't announce you want to move to Helena. I recognized that gleam in your eye when we were sightseeing earlier. I felt your interest in that college under construction on the hill. I know you have a desire to teach medicine some day.

Amelia shook her head slowly. *When he goes for walks early in the mornings, where does he go? Who does he talk with?*

BROADWATER HOTEL AND NATATORIUM, HELENA, MONTANA

~27~

The Broadwater Hotel and Natatorium

The week had passed quickly, and Amelia could see that her mother was tired after a morning's worth of sightseeing and visiting with Amelia's old friends. She decided it was time to make inquiries about another tourist attraction she had heard about just the day before.

"Excuse me, sir." Amelia called attention to her needs at the front desk of the hotel. "I'd like some information about the Broadwater Hotel and Natatorium. Can you help me?"

"Why, yes, of course I can assist you. What is your question?"

"I want to know where to make reservations and if we could stay several days starting today. We have been playing the visitor and we are exhausted. The Natatorium sounds like a lovely plunge, and I would enjoy a canoe ride on the lake with the swans floating beside me."

"Ah, yes. That does sound delightful. I might have to check in there myself one of these days." The two people laughed while the clerk searched for a leaflet about the resort.

"Here we are." He opened the leaflet before handing it to Amelia. "I can send a bellhop out there and make the arrangements for you. He has a bicycle and makes very good time."

Amelia studied the black and white printed paper. "I would like that very much.

We would need reservations for one single room for Joseph, another one single room for Josie . . . let's see, that takes care of . . . wait, we need another single for Sarah Marie, then put Mother and myself in a double room." She counted the rooms on her fingers and realized she was one short for Beulah. "I will need a servant's guest room, as listed here for Beulah." Amelia paused as if in thought. "Yes, that would cover us all." She looked at the hotel clerk. "Please make the reservations for five nights starting tonight."

The clerk made a note of her requests and told her the price per night would be $2.50 per person, and that included the mud baths. Meals would be added costs for each item on the menu. Amelia would pay those at the end of the five days.

"Splendid. Please give this greenback to the bellhop as a TIP." She handed him the bill.

"We prefer gold or silver coin over the greenbacks, Ma'am. But we will accept them if need be, seeing as you have come from Virginia."

"Thank you for that information. I'll try to make it to Thomas Cruse's bank today and pay you in full at checkout time." Amelia started to walk away from the counter, but stopped and went back to the clerk.

"I want to hold the rooms we have here for the month, even though we will be gone a few days. I don't want to have to take our entire luggage from here. There would be no room for us as passengers in the buggy we have rented."

The clerk laughed. "Ma'am whatever arrangements you need, we will see they are followed through." He had been doodling on a piece of paper. He handed it to Amelia.

"Here is a map for your son to follow to take you out to the Broadwater, as it is a short drive west of town." He looked down to the desktop, as if through talking to Amelia.

"One more thing. When you arrive at the State Nursery you will see a wonderful display of trees and flowers and shrubs. The public is invited to stop and walk inside the glass-topped buildings, and I have heard it is worth your time to the visit there on one of your days at the hotel." He paused. "The Mills family still owns and operates the business." He waved his hands in the air. "Most all of the trees you see planted in Helena came from that nursery."

"Why, thank you very much. We are having a lovely time revisiting Helena after being away for so many years. This hotel had just been on the drawing board when we left here, and there was construction for buildings, houses, sheds, warehouses . . . you name it."

Amelia touched her cheek before she pointed her index finger at the young man. "You can't believe the noise . . . night and day . . . from the hammers, and equipment being used for that work, and all of that was on top of the blasting from the mines in the hills surrounding Helena."

A smile spread across her lips as she realized she was reminiscing with a young man probably not as old as her son. He would have no interest or even understand what it was like 'back then when his parents came west,' and he had probably heard all of their stories for years. She noticed him yawn.

"I've detained you long enough. We will have our breakfast in the dining room and then start the drive out to the Broadwater Hotel and Natatorium . . . I like saying that name."

Amelia turned to see her family waiting to enter the dining room and was pleased everyone was up and ready for another day of excitement. She would tell them about her surprise move while they ate a hearty Montana cowboy breakfast of scrambled eggs, bacon cut thick, biscuits and gravy, beans, fried potatoes, toast, juice fresh squeezed that morning, milk, and delicious real roasted bean coffee. Her mother preferred tea with her meals, and she faithfully ate oatmeal served with whatever fruit was in season.

The black buggy clipped along at a rather fast pace as the graveled road was well maintained and flat. It seemed that they were leaving town and driving west into a wild land, when suddenly a row of cottonwood trees came into view. Amelia read the fancy sign advertising the State Nursery Company just down the lane.

"Joseph, slow down. This must be the turnoff road up to the right." Amelia pointed to a lane that ran between two whitewashed posts standing like guards for all passing buggies and other means of transportation.

"Oh, sister, look at that Russian style building." All eyes were staring into the field at the domed, long and narrow building. "That is the natatorium."

The horses continued along the lane. The Broadwater Hotel spread out right in front of them. "There, Mother." Amelia pointed toward an unusual style of design that gave the feeling of a fairyland." Look at that wooden structure with the turrets at each end. Why it is so modern looking. I heard that the doorknobs are coated in real gold."

Joseph chuckled as he listened to the women, their voices rising with every discovery. Peony bushes, in full bloom spilled out onto wooden walk paths that lead to a rose garden, their perfume reaching into the breeze that greeted them. Iris, standing grand and tall, vied for attention with bearded petals of copper and deep purple.

Sarah Marie squealed with delight at the wild birds perched in pine trees, huge cottonwood trees; species whose names she did not know. "Look at the robins flying over their nest. She must be feeding babies before teaching them to fly away." Bluebird houses were tacked along the white painted picket fence. Everything looked so unique no matter where she set their eyes.

Joseph took note of a lake behind the structure. He watched swans floating effortlessly across the water, their necks arched so perfectly, and the crowns on their heads giving them a look of royalty. Colorfully painted flat-bottomed canoes were pulled up to the dock, waiting for passengers, their oars carefully crisscrossed inside the boat.

"Joseph, I'll check on our reservations while you bring in the luggage." Amelia grabbed her own small satchel and that of her mother. With her reticule hooked over her left arm, she looked rather clumsy as she walked up the few steps leading in to the lobby.

Meticulously carved spindles and wood frame doors delighted the group. A fancy bell sat on the desk counter and Amelia gave it a tap. A leaflet listing the activities was open on the counter. Amelia picked up four copies so they could all read about what to do for the next few days.

Sarah Marie wished her daughters could be enjoying this wonderful vacation right along with her, but there wasn't the money or the time they could take away from their ranch chores at this time of the year. She would take her brochures that she had started collecting, and tell them about her special time with her mother, sister, Beulah and nephew Joseph. She looked around the group and said a silent prayer. "Thank you, Lord."

A bellhop took them to their prepared rooms. "Dinner will be served in one hour. Tonight we are featuring prime beef with vegetables of the season grown in the Chinese Gardens, and a strawberry-rhubarb custard cobbler that I am sure you will all want to taste." He expected a TIP as he held out his hand to Joseph.

Beulah was beside herself with joy. *For me to be wakin' up in this luxury for the next four days is pure heaven.* Servants' quarters, although not flamboyant with gold door knobs like the special guest rooms, were certainly adequate for Beulah's needs. The quarters were separated from the main hotel at the end of a long hallway, but actually located in an attached building.

I can empty my own chamber pot, and I have a pitcher and bowl to wash my face in the morning. Why, this is like bein' in high cotton. Beulah gave herself a hug before falling backwards onto the rope-tied mattress.

I must ask for a set of rules for the "servants" the next time I am in the lobby. They probably don't think I can read or write. They might have given a set of rules to Miss Amelia and she jess hasn't passed it on to me yet. Maybe at dinner time she will. Beulah would be allowed eating privileges in the kitchen, and enjoy the same meals as prepared for the guests. She would join the family after the meal for a stroll.

Beulah had her parasol and was ready to walk the grounds. Sarah Marie hurried to Beulah's side.

"Wait for me, Beulah. Let's walk over to the Natatorium and check out that plunge." Beulah wondered if she would be allowed to swim in the water but kept her thoughts to herself.

"I want to take a canoe ride, too. Can you imagine us floating among swans?" Sarah Marie's thoughts once again turned to her daughters working so hard on the homestead while she played. "I know I should feel guilty, but I don't, Beulah. This is my first vacation since my honeymoon, and not even rain for four days would dampen my spirits." She sighed as she turned to face Beulah. "Let's not waste a minute of our time together."

The walk across the grounds proved to be a wonderful sight. Benches were placed every few feet for their seating pleasures if they came upon a flower they wished to examine more fully. The two women marveled at the ever-bubbling fountain in the center of a cultivated lawn being vacuumed clean by a band of white sheep.

A post board caught their attention and Sarah Marie read the daily activities.

"We are just in time, Beulah. Tonight there is to be a concert presented by an all-black 56 piece band. Public invited. Hmm! We must remember to tell the others about this concert." She continued to peruse the program.

"Isn't it wonderful what the printing press has done for the territory?" As usual, Sarah Marie brought up historical events that had happened after Beulah and Amelia had left the community. "When the press began working in Virginia City, it spread news faster than two old biddies talking over the back fence." Beulah laughed. "Well, laws, we always will like good gossip Sarah Marie. What are you reading about now?"

"Tomorrow there will be tennis lessons, croquet games on the manicured lawn to the west, and a photographer located at the fountain for us to have our pictures taken for souvenirs. We must all do that so we can show Jack and the girls what a wonderful place this is, and that I am having such a good time." Sarah Marie tossed her hands into the air. "I will promise to some day bring the girls here, when the crop comes in, the bills are paid, and we still have life in our bodies." Laughter filled the air and floated along the walkway mixing with the perfumed smell from the roses.

"I want to try the mud bath in the morning, soaking up all the healthy benefits we can. Beulah. We must find out what you can participate in with us. Let's go and talk to someone at the front desk who can give us that information. I am not going to have you embarrassed at every turn while here."

Beulah gave a wan smile. "Missy Sarah Marie, jess bein' here with all of you is treat enough for me. Your family has never noticed my skin is a different color than yours, and I know being with Dr. Amelia has opened many doors not available to other coloreds . . ."

Sarah Marie cut her off. "Enough of that kind of talk. Beulah, let's go to the plunge, check out the facilities, and make our plans for the next few days."

She walked backwards, a few steps in front of Beulah.

"You want to know a secret?"

"What you goin' to tell me?"

"My sister is paying the whole bill for this trip and I don't feel a bit guilty about letting her do it. She has made a very good income over the years, living in the family home, using Father's offices for her own. She's always had luxurious surroundings to live in, maids, cooks, la-dee-da stuff and parties." Sarah Marie twirled around in her cotton gown and brown lace-up boots. "Nope. Not one bit, not one twinge, no guilt, just pure enjoyment and gratitude." She did a little dance step.

"But wait until you folks see where and how I live next week." She laughed. "Amelia and Mother will be shocked. I intend to dress Joseph in farmer clothes and send him into the field to help his Uncle Jack." She giggled and Beulah just stared at her, open-mouthed.

"Why laws, Sarah Marie. You little scamp. You ain't changed from that mischievous little girl from Virginia have you?"

The two women opened the extra wide and heavy natatorium doors and gazed in pure delight at the over-sized, warm water plunge. Sarah Marie clapped her hands over and over as she swept the entire scene with her eyes. "We have stepped into a jewel box, Beulah. Look at the windows . . . stained glass so rich in colors and reflecting in the water at our feet." Beulah was speechless.

"Never in a million years will my girls believe my stories about this plunge." Sarah Marie turned to Beulah once again. "Let's not tell Amelia and Mother about what we have seen. It has to be experienced firsthand. Joseph is a medalist swimmer and has been in many plunges, but I can guarantee you he has never swum in a jewel box before."

There is Flattery in Friendship.
William Shakespeare

~28~

Journey Begins

Sarah Marie and Amelia stood together admiring a bed of peonies. "As wonderful as the time spent at the Broadwater has been, Amelia, I'm missing Jack and the girls, and home." Sarah Marie flashed a winsome smile at her sister. "I'm so grateful to you for this vacation you have created for all of us. I'll remember forever seeing . . . ."

Amelia interrupted her in mid-sentence. "We will be together more often, Sarah Marie. Now that the railroad is complete and the trip isn't so long and arduous, we will make plans to keep connected." She put her hand on her sister's arm. "There is always a way to make things happen. You remember that."

The two sisters hugged briefly, and then returned to their chores.

Sarah Marie handed up yet another suitcase to Joseph who was stacking them tightly in the rear of the buggy for the trip back to the Grand Central Hotel, and the rooms reserved for them. They intended to sort through their clothes and leave in storage at the hotel the frivolous items, extra dresses, feather hats, things they would not be using on the farm.

Joseph had inquired into a small trailer-type wagon, and indeed, such a wagon was available. All of the luggage would be placed there. Sarah Marie had items from a list that Jack had asked her to purchase from the mercantile, hoping the order would be filled in time for her to bring the needed supplies when she returned.

The load would not be too much for the two horses, as they were used to pulling large loads. The animals were owned by the Wells Fargo Stage Company and were well trained for pulling wagons and buggies. A water barrel was strapped around a supporting metal pole. A sack of oats and wooden buckets hung on pegs on the outer side of the buggy.

Joseph spent time every day recording in a journal. He wanted to savor their movements, conversations, observations, and events that he participated in on this journey back into his Mother's past.

Whenever he had free time, Joseph read what he had written the night before. While waiting for the buggy to be loaded for the trip to the homestead, he pulled out his black book from his vest pocket. He licked the end of his lead pencil and he began to write:

> *The buggy is large and roomy. The seats are*
> *covered in leather, probably cow hide. A very large*
> *canopy fits well over the top and will provide some*

shade. Good springs give a bounce to the wheels making it not too uncomfortable.

The group plans to leave before daylight in order to take advantage of the cool morning air. We have nearly sixty miles to cover and will stop in the canyon the first night.

At Wolf Creek mother plans to renew old friendships with the Hicks family. We will probably stay overnight, continuing in the early morning hours of the next day. Auntie says we will be at the homestead before noon on the third day.

The first observation I made upon arrival was that during the summer time, first light arises over the Prickly Pear Valley way before 5:00 a.m. and a hot sun sneaks in on us by 10:00 a.m. Sunlight lasts until 10:00 p.m. This is called twilight. I am told this remains until the fall season.

*First frost occurs usually by September 15*th*. Snow has been known to fall by then, too. Hopefully, the harvest is in the barn.*

Joseph rested his hand.

Farming began with first light and ended when darkness overtook the crew in the fields. The hired hands were sunburned on any part of their bodies not covered with cloth. A farmer tan stayed with them year 'round showing their hat line. A bib-overall strap was a giveaway line on their shoulders as well. The younger men took off their heavy work shirts and allowed the sun to tan their skin to show off to their lady friends in the cool of the evening.

It was during that long sunlight time, some called it twilight, that families would sneak away to the Dearborn River and fish. The children played with a stick and ball, and the ladies spread a blanket to read, or just dream lazily, as the water rushed by sending music to their tired ears. Their horses stood nearby, stamping a foot or shaking their manes and swishing their tails at the sting of a horsefly.

Fishing was a favorite pastime for young Jackie, and he planned to take Joseph to his secret fishing hole every chance they could break away. The girls were not going to occupy Joseph's every moment, no sir. Not if he could get to him first.

They would be sleeping in the hayloft. The women would take over the house for the duration. Having a male cousin come to visit was a rare event, and Jack planned to make the most of it.

He wondered if Joseph played musical instruments. Jack played the violin, piano, organ, trumpet, accordion, guitar, banjo, harmonica, just about anything that made a sound. He could pick up a violin and have hands clapping and feet tapping at the community get-togethers and church suppers, weddings. On occasion, he'd even play for a graveside funeral.

Women wore Prairie Madonna sunbonnets to provide some shade, since the material had a flounce that covered the front and sides and had a flap that fell down covering the neck. A farmer's wife was easily spotted in the mercantile.

As hard as she might try, wearing a bonnet, covering her arms, keeping gloves handy in her reticule, carrying an umbrella, soaking in milk water, and spending hard-to-come by extra pennies on creams did not hold back the wrinkles the dry air eventually produced on her weathered face. Sparkling bright eyes stared out from wrinkled faces even in the younger women. One had only to wander about town to see the differences in complexions comparing city dwellers to farm women.

Business men were blessed with the opportunity to stay inside their stores, rarely forced outside to work in the heat of the day. Wagons filled with freight usually arrived in the evenings and freighters did the unloading for deliveries to be made in the early morning hours.

Another thought came to Joseph and he quickly jotted it down.

> *A certain hum or rhythm runs through the town. People correspond to the continuity of day-after-day activities.*
>
> *Sunday church bells awake the faithful and a different kind of timetable is followed. Families gather for Sunday meals, after attending local church services.*
>
> *The food is prepared on Saturday, since Sunday is to be a day of rest. It is my observation that men and children are fed by miracles since the women are to "rest" also. Ha.*
>
> *How different this lifestyle is compared to mine in Virginia. So much I have taken for granted being raised in it. We have servants for everything. I am*

*blessed beyond measure to be in a comfortable home with everything provided for me. Yet, I am fascinated by this way of living. **I want it for me.***

Joseph set down his pencil to reread that last sentence. It astounded him that he had so boldly scrolled his subconscious desires for his own future. He quickly picked up the book and stored it in his vest pocket not wanting anyone to read his secrets.

"We have to make a stop at the mercantile, Joseph. Sarah Marie has a few items to check on before we leave town." Amelia helped her mother into the buggy and propped a pillow behind her backside. "I do hope the hotel doesn't mind my taking pillows, but we have such a long ride and, well, we are going to need them."

Joseph stared at his mother. Never had he seen such boldness in her demeanor. "This country does strange things to your brains, Mother. Will you blame Beulah for taking them if you get caught?"

Amelia stiffened. "Joseph, such a thing never crossed my mind. We'll return the pillows, and I'll pay for them if need be. Now, you just drive us on over to the mercantile, if you please."

The order was ready for Sarah Marie. She signed the company credit slip, promising payment with the first harvest.

The owner had a package for Josie. He handed it up into the buggy. Amelia looked around for a safe place to set the box.

"I also have some letters for Josie for her post office duties. You might as well take the sack and save her the trip. She'll be busy having you folks stop by as it is."

Amelia chuckled as she put the sack on the floor beneath her feet. She'd do some rearranging when they were out of sight of the town.

"Time's a wasting, Joseph. Everyone ready?"

Nods and a couple of "uh-hums" greeted Amelia as Joseph snapped the reins.

The little wagon lurched but stayed attached to the hitch on the back of the buggy. With every rut and bump in the road, a cacophony greeted them, and Joseph became aware of the many rhythms: the horses pace, the wagon wheels hitting the cross ruts, and voices in muffled conversation. The Prickly Pear Valley seemed to welcome them as they ventured north on another leg of this incredible journey.

Everything is right about this trip. The restlessness in me that I could never before identify is settling. Clarity is coming into my mind and soul. I can set up my medical practice here, maybe buy some land and farm, find the perfect woman and even teach medicine.

"Joseph . . . Joseph." Amelia shouted from her side of the buggy. "Would you please stop? We need water from this creek. Our water barrel is empty already."

Beulah had become very quiet as they entered the north hills. She was never sure just where Moses lived in his hidden cabin, but she knew it was in this vicinity. Joseph stopped at a trickle of a creek where some willow bushes provided a bit of shade. Beulah unpacked tin cups for water for everyone. She carried a bucket as she walked to the creek's edge.

I wonder if this is the turnoff for Sheep Creek. I remember him sayin' he was higher up the canyon, turnin' to the right at Sheep Creek to get to his place on Rose Creek. My feelin's are tellin' me this is the place, all right. I wonder if they ever caught the man who killed Moses, shootin' him in the back. Probably not.

"Here you go, Joseph." She handed him a cup full of cool water. "Remember my friend, Moses? Well, this is near the place that I'm thinkin' he had his cabin and where he hunted for gold. That little creek right there is supposed to be full of the shiny stuff, waitin' for the pickin." Beulah shivered, but not from being cold.

Cool water

~29~

The Hicks Family at Wolf Creek

"They're here, they finally made it!" Josie ran from the door of the mercantile where she had been watching the road that led into Wolf Creek. She flew outside and wrapped her arms around a column that held up the porch roof.

When she saw the buggy loaded with people and the little trailer heaped full of supplies, she burst out laughing.

"Hello, hello. At last you are here. I've been watching every day for your arrival. Jack and the girls stopped by on their way home over a week ago. He said you'd be along soon, and now here you are."

She noticed a very handsome young man as he jumped down and secured the horses to the hitching post. He seemed a bit bewildered at all the confusion from the women clambering out the side door of the buggy, not waiting for him to help them out. Even his grandmother was excited to meet this woman wearing a white pinned on apron over a calico blue and purple full skirted dress.

She wore a green visor on her head and had a pencil stuck behind her ear. A full head of brown-gray hair was held in a bun with a narrow pink ribbon wrapped around it.

The woman bypassed him and ran right into the arms of Amelia. The two women held each other tightly, and then burst into laughter. Josie pointed to the wagon.

"You have more supplies trundling along behind you than I brought on the whole trip out west. You plan on staying a while this time?"

Amelia laughed and joined arms with Sarah Marie. Her mother, linked to Sarah Marie's other elbow, smiled and held out her gloved hand for Josie to take. "I am the girls' mother. I've heard so many stories about you, Josie, I feel like you are family."

Josie waved off the compliment and reached out to shake hands with Joseph.

But it was Beulah she wanted to give a big hug. "Beulah, oh, how I've missed you over the years." Beulah wiped away a tear from Josie's cheek.

"Life played some funny tricks on all of us, didn't she?" Beulah couldn't help it. She had to envelop Josie into her bosom one more time. That was when she noticed the curly, red-haired little girl standing off to one side. She wore a big green bow in her hair and her stockings clung to her knees. Her black lace-up shoes tied at her ankles.

"Mama? Who are these people? How come they know you?" The little girl clung to a cat in her arms, its tail almost touching the ground.

"Come here, darling. These are my friends from a long time ago." Josie put her hands on Matilda's shoulders. "This is my daughter, Violet Matilda Hicks."

The child curtsied. "You can call me Tillie. Everybody does. Even my best friend, Mabel calls me Tillie at school."

Amelia took her hand and shook it. "Tillie it is. You can call me Miss Amelia.

Everybody at home does." Laughter filled the courtyard in front of the store.

Josie looked at Joseph. "Frank and Frankie are working in the barn out back. They will be along any minute since I am sure they heard the noise we are making. All of Wolf Creek must know by now that my special company has arrived."

The building housed the mercantile, but one section had been built to serve as an apartment for when Josie worked at the store. It was her home-away-from-home, and in the winter the family lived there.

The children attended the South Fork School, not too distant from Wolf Creek. She also served as the post mistress. A special counter with small pigeon holes was built into one wall. People came for their mail, did their shopping and gossiped all in one stop. Josie was very efficient at what she did. She was proud of the fact that she had been named the official Post Mistress by the United States Postal Department. A brass plaque hung on the wall with her name stamped in bold letters. It had been issued as an award for her years of service.

"Come inside and get out of the heat. Joseph, there is a water trough on the west side of the building and shade for the horses and buggy if you want to pull the team around."

She noticed the mail pouch hanging on the wagon's side peg. "I see you have my mail delivery, too. You might just hand that to me now." Joseph also gave her the wrapped package meant for her and her family.

Josie led the ladies into the building, beaming with pride, anxious to show off the business she and her husband Frank Hicks had built up over the years.

"We have so much to talk about. But first of all, you must be in need of some refreshment. Tillie, will you help me in the kitchen, please?"

"Yes, Mother." The child walked backwards through the parlor, not wanting to miss out on any of the conversation, and then she turned on her heels to enter the kitchen. She had helped make lemonade from fresh lemons earlier that day. She hurried out to the little spring house that the creek ran through and fetched the gallon jug of juice. It felt icy cold.

Matilda noticed her mother had set out her best glasses onto a silver tray, along with fancy napkins. She had also filled a plate with homemade cookies. She very carefully walked back into the parlor. Each person took a glass, a napkin and a cookie as Matilda played the perfect hostess.

"Thank you, Tilda," Beulah said.

Matilda shook her curls. "'Tilda' . . . I like that name."

She stared right at Beulah. "I didn't know my mother knew any *black* people."

Josie whirled around at the comment and blushed a deep crimson. "Why, Matilda Hicks. Whatever made you say such a thing?" She started towards the girl, but Beulah intercepted.

"Oh! My laws! Am I black? Here I am an old lady and I never noticed my skin was any color than like yours. Now, how do you suppose the good Lord mixed me up like that?" Beulah frowned as she eyed the frightened child.

"Mama." She ran to her mother, still balancing the cookies on the plate.

Beulah gave a big belly laugh. "Honey child, I have black skin because my mama and daddy were African slaves. I was born in Virginia years before the Civil War." Beulah paused but only for a moment. "Surely you have studied about that terrible war, haven't you?"

Tilda nodded her head, but remained silent.

"Well, one of the reasons for that war was so we folks with black skin could be free to do things like learn to read and write, and have jobs and families just like you do.

You being born out here in the west makes all the difference 'cause you jess don't get to see many black folk here in your little town." Beulah didn't touch the girl's hair, although she wanted to soothe her.

"Your question was all right to ask and I'll answer it." Beulah looked at Amelia and Josie standing next to the window, both wearing a worried frown.

"It's a long story and by the time we have visited, you are a smart girl and you will have put the puzzle all together.

"I met your mama some twenty-five years ago and we helped start that big town you call Helena. Everybody came into the territory to find a new life, find gold, and not one person was a native born. We all came from somewhere else." She pointed to Joseph. "Now, he was born in Helena, so that gives him special rights, come to think of it. We all are transplants except him." Joseph smiled at her.

"But, before that, I grew up in the house of Miss Amelia and we jess been friends our whole life long." Beulah thought a minute.

"You know, I don't think Miss Amelia ever asked me how come my skin is black, and I know I never asked her how come her skin is white." She couldn't help herself when she added with a chuckle, "I guess we jess came out of the oven one not quite baked and the other a bit burned."

"That's about enough of that, Beulah," said Amelia. "You've traumatized her for life with that story."

The women were laughing at Beulah's joke. Tilda decided things were all right in her world once again. Joseph, however, wished the men would appear from the barn out back. He was about to ask for directions when Josie noticed he was uncomfortable. She gave Tillie a little push.

"Run out back and tell your Daddy and brother to come to the house and meet the company."

"Yes, Mama." The little girl was only too happy to escape.

South Fork School

Middle of First Row:
Matilda Violet Hicks

The Fishing Hole

~30~

Frankie and Joseph Meet

Within five minutes the parlor was filled to overflowing when two very muscular men, one older and one about Joseph's age, stepped inside, straw hats in hand. Josie did the introductions.

"Frank Hicks, meet Joseph Martin."

Joseph stepped forward, his hand extended.

"Frankie Hicks, meet Joseph Martin."

The younger man stepped forward and they awkwardly shook hands.

"Hello, it's nice to meet you both." Joseph turned to the older man. "I believe my grandfather bought the

Hicks Ranch in Virginia many years ago, probably when you moved out west."

Josie put one arm around Joseph's elbow and her other arm around Frankie's elbow. "You two boys were babies when we all came into the territory. Frankie had to sleep in the mercantile building the night you were born, Joseph."

"Funny, I don't remember that, Mama."

"Neither do I," said Joseph. The group laughed at the ease of the introductions.

"I do remember playing with you in the streets with a ball, however. Frankie, you had wooden toys that were the envy of all the other boys in the town."

"I still have those toys, too, don't I, Mama? Out in the shed on the homestead?"

The group continued to banter back and forth. Tilda watched, and listened in absolute awe that her sheltered world was growing more confusing by the minute. Her older brother, Frankie, was the oldest boy she knew and she looked up to him with pride for his skills and for how good he was to her. She listened carefully as plans for the evening meal were discussed. Then she heard her father suggest they go on a picnic that evening and try fishing in the river.

"Absolutely, I'd like to give fishing a try," said Joseph. "Since I have been busy with my medical clinic, I have not been fishing for several years. I brought some different boots and clothes hoping we'd do some wilderness camping while on this trip."

Josie could see that Mrs. Roberts was tired. She motioned to Amelia that they should unload their luggage and settle in for their visit.

"I have rooms ready for everyone for tonight. Nothing fancy, but adequate." Josie pointed to a row of little cottages across the street from the post office. "I rent out these cabins to fishermen." Josie turned to Frankie. "Would you show Joseph where to put the buggy and help him stable the horses?"

"Sure. Just follow me out back." Frankie stood up, stretched, and started for the kitchen door. Joseph followed him outside.

"I need to drop off the ladies' luggage first, and then we can take care of the horses and buggy." Joseph looked to the sky. "One thing, it doesn't look like rain, so our little tag-along wagon should be fine outside the building for the night, don't you think?"

After a rest in their little cabins, the tourists were eager to get outside and move around. The buggy ride had not been too strenuous, but everyone felt the need to stretch out their limbs.

Josie and Tilda put together a wonderful picnic spread of cold ham and beans, well water, homemade bread and apple pie. She gathered together several quilts, while Tilda packed silverware and plates. Pans and lucifers went into a wood box. They would send Frank to the homestead to hitch up their horses to the double tree and have the wagon ready. He was to load in some fishing gear since they would be camping alongside the Dearborn River. Frank planned to pack wood for a campfire to keep back the mosquitoes and deer flies that would surely attack them as the evening air cooled.

Joseph and Frankie were deep in conversation discussing the idea of living in the west and leaving all of the conveniences that the east offered.

Frankie was winning Joseph over with every sentence. "I just read that eighty percent of all homesteading families today are under the age of thirty." He glanced up to see Joseph's reaction. "Sure, the old folks were here a long time ago, but that first wave of homesteaders has either moved on or died. My folks are turning more and more of the farming over to me. Dad is getting stiffer with each spring crop. By fall, he's pretty stove up, and thinking about moving to California to live in the land of sunshine and oranges."

Joseph laughed. "I really don't see your folks as 'old,' Frankie. But then again, look at my mother. She is putting on the years as well." Joseph searched the picnic area for his mother. "She has had a very full and interesting life with quite the mixture of bitter and sweet." She waved to the two young men. "She has had a great medical practice and certainly made tremendous strides in helping younger women with their lifetime choices." He smiled as the two young men continued to talk.

Frankie looked Joseph squarely in the eyes. "Are you thinking of maybe moving out west?"

Before Joseph could answer, Tilda came running to his side.

"Hurry, the fish are jumping in the stream and we have a fire going. Mama brought a pan so we can cook what you two catch for our dinner." The little girl was so excited at having time to spend freely with company. She loved having the two young men tease her and pull her hair, now woven into braids.

"You're on, Tilda. Let's make a bet." He raised up five fingers. "I'm going to catch five fish in fifteen minutes." Frankie started running to the wagon to grab his favorite fishing pole. He had just purchased the latest line made out of silk, increasing his chances to win the bet.

While standing on the creek shore, Joseph thought back about their conversation earlier in the evening. *Would I be happy out here in the west? I am leaning more and more towards the idea of moving here maybe next year. Much will depend on how Mother feels about my leaving her practice. She had her wild adventure. Surely, she would not forbid me from having mine.*

The golden glow from the setting sun still held warmth. Beulah watched the two young men casting their silver lines in a rhythm that could have been set to music.

She saw the fish jump, leaving a ring of circles as they plopped back into the water. "Hurry and catch somethin'. We're waitin' here for all those fish."

She clapped her hands when she saw Josie uncover a cooked ham hidden beneath the white, heavy cotton dishcloth.

"Never mind, you two. I'm eatin' what Josie caught." Beulah laughed her deep contented laugh that meant she was happy to be right where she was this very evening.

She made her sandwich, poured a large jar full of water and sat down on a driftwood log. This was the best vacation she had ever had, or would ever have again, of that she was very sure. Age, creeping into Amelia and also into Beulah, came unannounced. It caught them by surprise just this past Christmas, and that's when the idea of coming west for one more adventure jelled in Amelia's mind.

Mrs. Roberts, delighted with all the new things she was seeing, hearing and feeling, expressed her delight as she bit into the homemade apple pie. "Why, Beulah, you must get this recipe. I think it is even better tasting than yours." She looked at Beulah who had cast her eyes toward the ground. Mrs. Roberts realized she had said the wrong thing and tried to soften the words. "It must be the apples you use, Josie. Will you share your pie making secrets?"

A tired, but happy bunch of travelers wound their way slowly back to the Wolf Creek house. They had their fill of fresh trout, and were content with the evening sunset. They listened to the jangle of the horses' harness. Tilda snuggled up next to Beulah to shake off the cool air and yawned. She had been a very energetic young girl since early morning and at last was winding down, actually looking forward to bed time.

Josie and Frank, also tired, knew they still had some chores to finish up before they could turn in. The horses would need tending. Amelia and Beulah offered to help with the cleaning up from the picnic.

Inside the house, Frank lit some kerosene lamps. The glow shining out through the windows, lit a little square of land, otherwise the yard was pitch black. A coyote yip yipped from a distant knoll. Josie's dog, lying on the porch, perked up his ears and answered the ancient mating call.

Table Mountain

~31~

The Frey Homestead

It seemed to Sarah Marie that their departure from the Hicks family was dragging out way too long.

After all, they will be back again visiting on the return to Helena, and Joseph and Frankie can talk then. I have a family and farm to tend. I am anxious to be on my way. Sarah Marie ran her hands through her hair.

"Joseph," she called out, "we must be leaving . . . Now! The horses have a long way to travel, and we want to make time in the cool of the morning." She smiled at her sister, and motioned her to move toward the buggy steps. "Come, help mother into the buggy."

Joseph reluctantly broke away from his conversation with Frank and Frankie. "We'll continue this discussion another day . . . very soon . . . but goodbye for now."

Little Tilda gave Beulah one last hug. "Thank you for my new name. I just love saying it to my friends." She looked up into Beulah's eyes. "I'll be waiting to see you again real soon."

Everyone climbed aboard, and the little trailer on back jangled as the horses pulled away from the mercantile building. They followed a well-traveled route back into the prairie grasses, headed north toward Augusta and the Frey homestead. Sarah Marie sighed with relief. Almost a week had passed and she was ready to end her vacation in Helena. It was time to get back to the summer chores she knew would be waiting for her hands.

The summer sun grew hotter as the day progressed. Amelia was happy she had remembered to pack parasols, one for each of them. The buggy had a partial covering with fringe hanging down the sides, but the relentless sun found ways to reach arms and necks and the delicate umbrellas were welcomed. "What a sight we must be with these bright parasols," said Beulah.

"Do you see many buggies, wagons, or even horses for that matter? I think we are quite safe from ridicule out here in the big open." Sarah Marie started twirling her bumbershoot and created a bit of a welcome breeze.

Every half hour Joseph stopped to rest the team and give them water. He'd look ahead searching to find a cluster of trees, but to his dismay, they were very few and far between.

"Sarah, how much longer will we be out in this country?" Her mother looked rather red faced and tired. "Amelia, have you ever been out on this range?"

Sarah interrupted. "The landscape from Ft. Benton is similar, Mother. This is cattle country. Oh! And be careful walking around in the tall grasses and sage brush. Rattlesnakes live out here in abundance." Sarah Marie tried to sound nonchalant about the rattlesnakes.

Beulah and Sarah Marie looked at each other and burst into laughter. "Do you remember Rattlesnake Hill on the north end of Helena?" Sarah was talking to Beulah, loud enough for the others to hear."

"Remember? My laws, Miss Sarah Marie. I more than remember. It seemed like every time we'd turn around, there'd be another one." She stopped to take a breath. "Remember the rule? If you find one, kill it; look around because if there is one there is another. They travel in pairs. That's why I never wanted to go out to the woodshed in the dark, for sure."

The grandmother shuddered and gasped at the same time. "Sarah Marie, you never wrote about dangerous snakes in all these years. Do you have them at your house, too?"

"Oh, yes, mother. We never go out into the grasses, around wood piles, or rock piles without carrying our long poles or hoes for the garden work. Why, I have had snakes curled up on our porch more often than I can count." She smiled at the passengers.

"You just learn to watch out for them and avoid gopher holes and try to stay on the back of your horse when a snake is around. They smell really bad and when they are coiled up they rattle their tails. They warn you, if they are not sunning themselves on a rock or something." Sarah Marie watched as every one of the passengers shrunk inside themselves just a little bit. She felt guilty.

"I bet you we don't even see one snake the whole time you will be at the homestead." Her words fell on deaf ears as every person had their eyes focused on the ground near the wagon wheels instead of watching the landscape change as Table Mountain came into view.

It was well on to noon when Sarah Marie jumped up in the buggy. "There!" She pointed. "Look over to the left and you will see the roof of our barn. We'll be there within twenty more minutes." A big smile spread over her face. "We're almost home."

"Here comes the buggy! Mom's home!

Sarah Marie saw her darling daughters come into view as the buggy rounded the top of a small hill and then dropped down the slope. The gate already swung open, held four young women standing on the bottom pole waving and shouting greetings to the company.

"Dad! Mom's home," Nora shouted towards the barn. "Grandmother Roberts and Auntie Amelia are riding in the rear and Beulah is up front pulling shotgun duty while Joseph is driving." Nora cupped her hands around her mouth to make sure her dad heard her calling him.

"They have a funny little wagon hitched to the back of the buggy." Suddenly, Jack Frey appeared by the side of the barn. He tossed the pitchfork from his hands back into the hay stack he was loading into the barn loft.

The girls swung the gate shut behind the buggy and Joseph made his way to the front of the barn. He eyed that pitchfork, thinking he would be needing it for a weapon very soon.

"Jump down, son, and stretch those legs and your arms. You have had a long drive in this heat." Joseph did exactly as he was told. Then the two men helped the women out of the buggy. Jack put his rough, calloused hand on Sarah Marie's shoulder.

"You've been sorely missed, Sarah Marie. But the girls have done a great job these past few days." He looked into her smiling face. "Did you have a nice visit?"

"Jack, it was marvelous, wonderful, and much too long for me to be away, but I will be forever thankful for being free to do so." She gave her husband a big hug and a kiss on his cheek. She then hugged each girl. "Where is Jackie?" she asked.

"Jackie is out cutting hay. He'll be in for supper when the bell's rung."

He pointed to the girls. "Help unload your mama's things, girls, and we'll get inside out of this heat."

Jack turned to Joseph and chuckled as he walked over to the wagon. "Let's get this unloaded, too, Joseph. We can unhitch it and pull it over to the granary yonder." He looked at the hodge-podge of supplies. "Looks like the mercantile had about everything on my list. Sure glad for that as Sarah Marie won't be going to town very soon again, what with the hay ready now, and grain ready for harvesting in a few weeks." He looked to the sky. "Sure hope we don't have a hail storm."

He pulled off his straw cowboy hat and wiped the sweat from his brow. Joseph noticed the white skin on Jack's forehead and for the first time realized what a "farmer tan" was all about. Jack's face was leathered by the sun over the years, and age had wrinkled his skin to put "character" into his countenance.

Joseph followed instructions and soon the two men had everything unloaded in the granary. He unhitched the buggy that had been pulled to the east side of the barn into its shade. The horses were put into a corral that also had shade for the rest of the day and evening hours. Jack wanted the horses to cool down a bit before giving them water.

Their new goal was to head for the wash basin and then enjoy a tall cold drink of good well water.

The dinner bell clanged for a full five minutes. Joseph looked off to the hay meadow when he heard the jangle of horse harness. Jackie had left the mower in the field. He rode one horse bareback, leading the other workhorse back to the barn. The sight was one Joseph would remember for years to come, as he watched man and beast both well-suited for their jobs.

It felt good to sit in the parlor area of the ranch house. Mrs. Roberts, however, was appalled at the living conditions her daughter endured out on this god-forsaken piece of land.

I must not criticize. She is making her way here and there is enough love and happiness to go around. So, who am I to speak out? But, my goodness, this is not what I expected, not at all. Virginia must seem like a dream to her after all these years of hard work and survival. I must be careful while here to not hurt her feelings, even if she brings it up for discussion. She took a sip of the cold water and sat on the hard-backed kitchen chair with all the southern charm she could muster. Her fan flapped in her hands, trying to cool her skin, but not doing a very good job.

She watched her granddaughters in their light cotton dresses and wished she could strip down to her skin.

Maybe she would ask Sarah Marie for a simple frock to wear.

Sarah Marie was so happy to be with her daughters. "Girls, I have brought you all a promise. Come here to me." Each girl received a postal card of the Broadwater Hotel and written on the back was a note from their mother.

> *"I promise we will vacation at this hotel in the very near future. You have to see it with your own eyes to believe the wonders of that magical place.*
> *Stained glass windows almost everywhere and food fit for kings at every meal. Swans float on a little lake, and I rode in a canoe, paddling right near the birds. We swam in a plunge in this huge natatorium and the water was hot at one end and cold at the other.*
> *Pray for a good crop this season.*
>
> > Love,
> > Mother

Mrs. Roberts put her hand to her mouth. She turned her head slightly as tears formed and threatened to spill onto her cheeks. *Why, I will make certain Sarah Marie has the money before we leave here to take her family on a vacation this fall. She has never asked me for a thing all these years, and I didn't know she wanted for things.*

Amelia must be as shocked as I am at the conditions they are living in.

"Come to the table, everyone. Supper is set." The voice startled Mrs. Roberts back to reality and they all trooped to the round kitchen table. They easily fit in a tight circle. Fried chicken cooked earlier in the wee morning hours, cold potato salad and steamed vegetables, homemade breads, butter, and dollops of fresh cream were plopped on top of a rhubarb cobbler; milk, tea, coffee, and water filled the table as dish after dish was passed from left to right.

The guests had not eaten since early morning and the sight of the cooled food, companionship and conversation satisfied their hunger pains. In unison, they erupted into laughter every time Jackie would say, "Pass the chicken, please."

"My goodness, how do you ever concoct such wonderful salads with hardly any kitchen utensils to use? Where is your ice box? For that matter, where is your ice?"

Elsie blurted out, "We don't have any ice. But we have a root cellar. We make root beer and store it in the cellar. I'll show it to you after a while." Elsie blushed at her boldness.

Beulah smiled. "I'd like very much to see where you store your supplies, but do you have an extra stick for me to carry when I am outside to keep back the rattlesnakes?"

"What?" asked Gertrude. "Who has been filling you with stories like that? MOM! It had to be you." Sarah Marie laughed out loud. "Honey, I just couldn't help it. Once we got to talking about rattlesnakes, the stories just kept pouring out of my mouth."

Gertrude rolled her eyes. "Well, in my mom's defense, you do have to watch out for them, especially in this heat. This is wild country and they live here. Surely you have snakes in Virginia?"

Amelia spoke first. "Yes, we do, but they are not in our yard, thank heavens. We have gardeners who probably keep track of animals like gophers, and such. We live in a community, a village with lots of people, like in Helena."

Beulah didn't say anything, but she knew of the different types of snakes and other wild creatures her brother Rufus encountered while working on the Roberts property. He never wanted to scare any of the people living in the household since it was not often one came up from the nearby river.

Jack stood up. "Thanks for the good meal, daughters." He grabbed the back of his wooden chair. "We work from dawn to dark during these summer days." "Sarah Marie, you must show the guests to their quarters. I have to get back to the work at the barn. Joseph, if you have a hankering to stretch out, feel free to walk on over any time." Jack strode from the kitchen and the screen door banged shut behind him.

"Okay. Mother and Amelia, you will sleep in our bedroom. Beulah will have Jackie's bed. I'll bunk on the trundle bed with Nora Bee. That way the house will be a "hen" house with just us girls." They all laughed and looked at Joseph.

"Joseph, you and Jackie and Jack are banished to the barn for the duration. We have a hayloft guest house waiting for you. Actually, it is quite comfortable when the evening breezes finally work up and blow through the open windows high up in the barn." She winked at her nephew. "A rooster will wake you in the first light of day tomorrow."

The Frey Family

Fresh Rhubarb Pie

For best pie, chose early rhubarb stems, tender and pink. Do not peel. Cut into 1 inch pieces (1 lb. makes 2 cups.)

Amount of sugar depends on tartness of rhubarb. Early rhubarb requires less sugar. Make your pie shallow. Make pastry for two-crust pie. Line pie pan.

Filling
Mix 1 to 2 cups sugar
With ½ cup Gold Medal flour.
Mix lightly through 4 cups rhubarb.
Pour into pie pan.
Add top. Cut slits in it. Cut off overhang.
Time: Bake 40 to 50 minutes in hot oven.

From the recipe book of
Sarah Marie Frey
This recipe also makes rhubarb sauce for pancakes or for cobblers.

Barn on Frey Homestead

Granary on Homestead

Jack Frey and Lamb

The true sign of intelligence is not knowledge but imagination.

Albert Einstein

~32~

Morning Comes Early

Just as Sarah Marie predicted, a huge rooster crowed three times. "Cock-a-doodle-doo, Cock-a-doodle-doo, Cock-a-doodle-doo."

Joseph peeked through half-shut eyes out into the barnyard and he saw the rooster, puffed up, filling his daily job of waking everyone up. Streams of sunlight made a pattern inside the loft where the weathered boards had dried, leaving narrow slits between the vertical boards. The one unshuttered window told Joseph it was daylight.

I wish I had some rocks to throw at him. Joseph swung himself out of the hay mound. He looked around for his boots and clothes, only to find a pair of worn farmer boots, thick handmade wool socks, heavy work pants and a shirt lay out at the foot of his hay bed. He looked around for Jack and Jackie. Not seeing them,

Joseph put on the clothes, surprised that they were big enough for him.

Joseph heard a swishing sound coming from the main floor of the barn. He scooted down the wood ladder, landing near a huge dairy cow wearing the longest eyelashes he had ever seen.

"Well, sleepyhead, you finally woke up? Did old MacDonald get you stirred up and out?" Joseph found Jackie sitting on a short, one-legged stool with a bucket underneath the cow. He was pulling on the teats, squeezing fresh milk from the cow's enormously full bag.

"Want to take a try at milking?" Jackie stood up, allowing Joseph to take his place.

"Why not? That doesn't look too difficult to master . . . is it?" He saw some feral cats circling the floor by the cow. Joseph carefully slid onto the stool. "Okay . . . now I just pull down?"

Jackie smiled. "Well, for starters, Old Bess here is pretty friendly so she won't kick at you, but just the same, watch out for her hind hooves to come up suddenly. She swipes at flies that way, too."

Joseph tugged a few times but nothing happened.

"You got to give her a punch on her bag to get the milk flowing again."

Joseph did as instructed and sure enough, the swish, swishing sound hit into the bottom of the bucket. The cats came closer and one put his paws onto Joseph's knee, his mouth facing the cow's bag.

"Turn your spigot toward the cat. He wants a drink."

Joseph tried to aim for the cat's mouth and the cat swallowed the warm milk. He hopped down, and another took his place. Joseph paid close attention, but laughed as the cats returned again and again. "Enough of this. We need that fresh milk to make cream and butter, right Jackie?"

"Right. Mother needs a couple of gallons every day to keep up with all I drink at every meal." Jackie took the bucket away so that Old Bess did not kick it over. He led her outside into the grassy meadow to the east side of the barn where her calf was bawling for her. "Thanks, old girl. See you this evening."

"You do this twice a day? Every day?"

"Yep. We don't get days off from our chores. For Mother to take off those few days must have seen sinful to her, knowing all the work that had to be done. But Dad wanted her to have this time to spend with her own mother and sister and to relive a bit of her youth." Jackie sighed. "Someday I hope all of my sisters get to see some of this world. As for me, I am content right here on the farm. I have everything I need and want . . . right here."

Joseph followed Jackie to the house. He was surprised at all the activity and noise. The smell of hot coffee, bacon and eggs, and warm pancakes greeted the two young men before they opened the screen door.

"You look good in farmer clothes, Dr. Martin." Elsie giggled as she handed him a bar of lye soap and a bucket of warm water. "You can wash up over here in the wash room."

Everyone gathered around the huge table and Sarah Marie asked Joseph to say a prayer for their meal and for safety throughout the day as they went about their chores.

The words came easily to him; how genuinely happy he felt on this glorious summer day.

"Do you have chores for me?" Joseph turned to his uncle. "I'm a fast learner. I milked a cow today without spilling over the bucket. That is a real achievement, wouldn't you say?" He looked at the smiling face of his grandmother.

"As a matter of fact, I need you in the hayfield. We have it cut flat, and it has to be raked into a windrow. Then we rake the windrow into small stacks. Tomorrow, we'll use the horses and hay wagon. You'll pitch the hay into the wagon and take it to the stacks . . . near the old stacks of hay you see out in the fields." Jack looked at the bewildered young nephew sitting across from him. "I stack the hay. I'm particular. Come next winter the hay gets frozen solid if not stacked a certain way."

"Don't worry. Jackie and I will show you what to do. You know how to handle horses very well, and it is no different with a workhorse." He smiled. "In fact, our horses are so used to their jobs, they will tell *you* what to do, and all you will have to do is hold on to the reins." Laughter erupted around the table.

"Sarah Marie, fill this man up with your sourdough pancakes and black coffee. We've got work to do." Joseph did not need a clock to tell him it was still very early. "The sun wakes up early out here in the west, and it keeps shining very late into the evening, too." Joseph said, as he yawned and took another gulp of coffee.

"We take advantage of that sunlight, and we put in some hard days. Sarah Marie makes me take off most Sundays as a day of rest. That's the Lord's day. I pray we don't get hailed on come a Sunday." Jack put down his fork. "Those cows don't wait 'til spring to be fed." With that, he wiped his mouth on a square of cloth and jumped to his feet.

"Come out when you are ready. Jackie will be in the barn harnessing up the horses, and I'll be in the repair shop just down the road going towards the hay meadow."

Before Joseph could respond, he heard the slamming of the screen door. The kitchen table had two empty chairs around it, and one by one the women began clearing away the dishes.

Beulah was already washing dishes in a hot tub of water sitting on a side table. There was steam rising out of a pan of water set on the hot stove. His mother and grandmother had left by a side door to take a walk in the fresh morning air.

I'm about to find out what tired muscles really feel like, I've got a feeling. Come sundown, I'm going to be ready to "hit the hay". He chuckled as he thought about his bed in the barn. *What a story I will have to tell my friends back home. They'll never believe the renowned physician, Dr. Joseph Martin, milked a cow, put up hay, pitched manure, and loved every minute of it.*

Joseph found the repair shop. His uncle sat on a very small seat in front of a huge spinning grindstone wheel, holding a homemade sickle blade. It looked dangerously sharp. His feet were pumping up and down on pedals connected to the spinning wheel. "Want to try the wheel?"

"I think I'll pass on that chore. I have to be careful of my hands for when I do operations." Joseph looked at his hands and was grateful for them. He had become a very skilled surgeon. The clinic his grandfather had established was well-stocked. Joseph had the latest medical equipment to make his job much more precise.

Patients came from many miles around the village because of his reputation as a reliable physician. His mother had established a clientele over the years, winning the trust of their patients.

Joseph liked . . . no, loved . . . his life as a doctor. Helping people who were sick or injured filled his days. Unless called upon to do so, he left birthing babies to Beulah and his mother.

"Grab that leather strap and follow me," said Jack. "I've got a break in some harness that has to be fixed before Jackie gets here with the team."

"Do you go like this, like a house on fire, every day, sir?"

"Most days, yes . . . winter time, not so much. Each season brings different chores. Spring is plowing and seeding. Calves come night and day for a while, and then we have to brand the new calves." Jack looked at his nephew and saw genuine interest in the life of a homesteading family.

"Summer is gardening, canning, haying. Come fall we will harvest the grain, go into the woods and cut trees to chop into stacks for our wood supply. A trip to Augusta, not too far from here, will get us kerosene for the lamps, and the many supplies Sarah Marie has marked on her list." Jack paused. "Come winter, that's when we feed cattle all that hay you are going to work on today. I also spend time here in the workshop repairing things for spring."

"There is a rhythm to farm life, son. We follow the sun, the seasons, the harvests, and whatever the good Lord sends our way."

Jack stopped talking, absorbed in trying to think how he was going to make that leather strap fill in the tear. He took a handful of short rivets and a punch from the shelf over his work bench. "I'm going to do some operating of my own, Joseph. Stand back and watch."

Jack punched holes into both pieces of leather, and then he placed the two pieces together in a straight line, matching the holes. He put the rivet into the hole, placing it all onto an anvil. He hammered down hard, smashing the rivet. He turned over the leather strap. One more blow of the hammer brought the rivet down into the leather, holding the two pieces securely tight. He repeated the steps on the other end of the strap. He picked up his project and pulled hard. It did not break . . . and he smiled.

Jackie and the horses filled the open door frame. The two men placed the horse collar over the horses' necks and tossed the harness over their backs, attaching it all to the wooden double tree bar that stretched across the front of their chests. The wagon tongue split the team.

"See you in the field." Jackie waved to them as he trotted behind the eager horses. The wagon sat in the hay meadow and he would hitch the team to it. His straw hat, torn in a few places, had a sweaty band. *A kind of badge*, thought Joseph.

Following his uncle's lead, Joseph looked to the sky. Clouds were briskly crossing the heavens. "We have to work fast, today, Joseph. I'm very thankful you are here. We don't need hail on our hay, and the grain is about to head out. So, say a prayer those clouds keep right on moving."

It didn't take Joseph long to learn how to follow behind the horses and toss pitchfork loads of hay into the wagon box. Sweat poured from his head and his hat was soon sopping wet. Rivulets of sweat rolled behind his ears and into his eyes.

Before Joseph had left the kitchen, Nora Bee had dipped a red kerchief into the water bucket. She had handed it to him.

"Be sure and tie this around your neck and when you get into the field, tie it around your hair just under your hat brim. It will keep you cooler." She also handed him a canteen made from heavy canvas. It was filled with water. "You can pour some of this water over your kerchief, but don't waste it. You have to drink water all day long, too."

Joseph kept his kerchief wet, tried to keep the sweat out of his eyes, and kept forking the dried grass. He was no sissy. He'd show them he could put in a day's work right along with them.

It isn't even ten o'clock and I am aching in every muscle, joint, limb in my poor body. How do they do this day after day? I have a new respect for the farmers. Never again will I take for granted the produce in the village grocery store, never mind the milk in the coolers and the ice cream and butter and heavy cream for my coffee . . . and the work the hired hands do for us . . . I'll never see a beefsteak on my plate in the same way. To think it all depends on the weather nature sends. Farming is blind trust in the Lord, if ever I witnessed it.

When the noon bell clanged, a very tired young man limped slowly back up the hill to the house. Celine greeted him with a large Mason canning jar full of cold well water. She had the bar of lye soap and a towel for him, along with a huge bowl of warm water to wash his hands and face.

Joseph noted Jack and Jackie followed suit. "Ah! That is the most luxurious bath tidying up I have ever had the pleasure to experience." He did not mention that the lye soap burned his eyes, already red from the sweat he endured during the morning.

"Good work, son. After lunch we'll let the horses rest a bit and we'll do the same." He pointed to the north side of the barn. "There'll be some shade there."

Jackie, Grandmother and Grandad

~33~

Christmas in July

Amelia closed the Shakespearian book she found on the shelf in the parlor when she realized that Nora Bee stood quietly by the side of her chair.

"Yes, Nora Bee? Is there something you want to ask me?"

Nora Bee rubbed her left arm with her right hand, and then wiggled a bit next to her aunt. "We were wondering if . . . if you'd like to make Christmas decorations with us."

Amelia took off her gold wire-rimmed reading glasses and set them on the table. "Why, that is a wonderful idea. Yes, I'd like that. We can have us a Christmas dinner and decorate the house and table. Then I can take some of the decorations with me and put them out in December to remind me of all of you . . . of this." Amelia stood up. "What do you want me to do?" She mused. "Oh! I'll go find the others to join in."

Nora Bee giggled and twirled around. "Just a minute. I'll be right back." Off she went to the bedroom to find her sisters waiting behind the half shut door.

"What did she say, does she want to do it?" asked Elsie.

"Oh, yes, she does. She is going to go and find Beulah and Grandmother. We can put string, crayons, paper and glue, and . . . and ribbons out on the kitchen table. Let's start working right now."

The girls found the craft supplies in a wooden crate. They added scissors to the box. Several round white paper doilies with lace trim stuck out from the variety of papers stored in the box. Sarah Marie carefully kept all used wrapping paper and found many uses for it.

"This will be fun. We can make snowflakes and stars and dip them in wax." Celine had already cleared off the table and put down a piece of oilcloth for a cover. She made sure there were enough chairs for everyone to sit comfortably while they worked.

Beulah came in from the kitchen where she had been writing out some of her favorite recipes, and Grandmother Roberts put down the old sweater she had been unraveling. Sarah Marie wanted the yarn to make a pair of mittens for one of the girls. Everything was recycled that came to the homestead, some items more than once.

Gertrude reached for a ruler and pencil. She grabbed wrapping paper that had been saved from the Christmas before. Red bells, bright green wreaths and striped candy canes were printed on it.

"I'm going to make a six-pointed star." She turned the paper over to draw straight lines on the back side. With her scissors she cut long and narrow strips.

"I want to make a paper chain," said Nora Bee. She found papers in solid colors: red, green, yellow and blue. Following her sister's lead, she also made long strips with the ruler and scissors.

"Now, I need the paste. She called out to Elsie who was standing at the dry sink. "Do you have the flour and water paste ready yet?"

Elsie set a bowl full of a sticky glob mix on the middle of the table. She had wooden sticks to use, but Amelia noticed the girls were more comfortable using their index fingers to spread the glue on the strip ends.

Soon the table top was covered with circles. Nora Bee carefully picked out circles and laid them in front of her space. She took strips and hooked two of the circles together, pasting the ends shut. In just a few minutes she had a chain that hit the floor, and she was not through yet. "I want this chain to be six feet long at least." The ladies cooed and awed and encouraged the girls with their projects.

Sarah Marie appeared with a large jug of homemade root beer and a plate of Beulah's oatmeal cookies.

"Take a break, everyone. Have a cookie right out of the oven. These cookies are Beulah's favorite recipe and there is a secret ingredient in them. Surprisingly, I had that ingredient in my cupboard, but I hardly ever use it." She smiled at the girls.

"Can you identify what you are eating?" She waited a minute. "Whoever does gets a prize." Every one took a cookie and munched away.

"I know . . . I know what it is." Celine raised her hand like she was in class.

"It's mint."

"Right you are my smart daughter. Your prize is, hhhmmm, you don't have to help with the dishes tonight."

"Yeah!" said Celine. "Boo!" said the others. Then laughter erupted all around the circle as they each took another cookie.

Amelia chose a doily to work with. She folded it over and over. She took scissors and made slits along the fold lines. Then she put paste on the two ends, holding it between her two fingers until she felt it had stuck together. When she gingerly lifted the paper, she fanned it open to show a perfectly round ball with lacy cutouts.

"Look at my fancy snow flake." She held it up high so everyone could see the delicate ornament. She took a ribbon and poked it through one end and tied a knot.

"Sarah Marie, this ornament is for you to hang up at Christmas time and remember our visit." She handed the delicate paper craft to her sister.

"Oh, please sign it for me," said Sarah Marie. "That is a keepsake."

Grandmother Roberts had an eye for the pieces of colored ribbon, surprised to see it in the bin. "In my day, we wore colored satin and velvet ribbons in our hair. Do you girls do that now-a-days?"

"I think we all still like to wear ribbon hair pieces, and we put brooches in the middle of a piece of ribbon and tie it around our necks. But these ribbon pieces that find their way into the craft bin are too short and really not good for anything," said Elsie.

Grandmother kept working her fingers over the piece of ribbon, pleating the strips into a circle, using the glue as she went, holding the ribbon with her other hand. "I beg to differ with you, Elsie, but look at what I just made."

She opened her hand. There sat a perfect flower, like rose petals floating around in a tight circle. The paste held it all together in the center. She took a piece of ribbon, bent it into a small circle, then added several thin strips of another color of ribbon to hang down the side. This she glued to the middle of the flower. She cut a small circle out of a piece of heavy cardboard and glued the flower to the paper.

"Now, when it dries thoroughly, we can attach a pin to the back of it. You can add a brooch and put some beads on the ribbon that is hanging down. You will have a beautiful flower around your neck, or you can pin it to your lapel. This can be added to a fancy hat, too."

Grandmother was very pleased with her flower. "I will make one for each of you girls and you can wear them Christmas Day." She looked at the assembly around the table. "Merry Christmas." She clapped her hands in her excitement.

All of a sudden, the girls starting singing. The chorus of voices brought a stillness to the room. "Silent night, holy night, all is calm, all is bright." Beulah added her deep voice to the chorus and stood up with the girls.

Amelia came to the choir next and looped her arm around her sister's waist. Soon everyone surrounded the table in a chain of song. Their voices carried outside through the open windows and doors. A gust of wind picked up the music sending it, as if planned, down the lane to the hay meadow.

"Do you hear singing? Christmas songs?" The three men stopped for a moment to listen to the comforting sound. For a moment in sacred time, the family united as one. "Should old acquaintance be forgot and never brought to mind . . ." sang Jack to the two men. Time stopped as Joseph leaned on his pitchfork. One of the horses nickered, breaking the spell. Work resumed.

Celine had been sitting very still as she patiently worked on her strips to make a three-dimensional pointed star. She folded and braided the strips making sharp points. Watching her delicate fingers working so deftly with the strips brought a smile to her grandmother's face.

"Why, I used to make those stars, only I never thought to dip them into paraffin to make them stay stiff." She stood up. "I'll go check the melting wax and see if it's ready." The wax had been set on the stove top in a pan of water. The heat from the oven where the cookies had been just a few minutes before had melted the wax. She carefully took the pan to Celine.

"Here you go. Let's see what happens next."

"Watch, Grandmother. See how the points make it nice and sharp? The star will sit on the table to decorate the turkey. I'm going to make a bunch of stars in different sizes and colored paper."

"Do you always have turkey for Christmas?" Beulah asked. "We have ham for Christmas, but turkey for Thanksgiving in Virginia."

Sarah Marie joined in the conversation. "We raise turkeys, so yes, we have turkey for Thanksgiving and Christmas dinners. I take them to Augusta for market, along with eggs and chickens."

The afternoon passed too quickly. A large pile of ornaments in various shapes and designs crowded the center of the table. It was time to clean up everything and get the dinner meal ready for the men who would be coming in very soon, hungry, dirty and tired.

"Aunt Amelia, would you take home one of my stars, please? I signed it, too." Celine chose the star for her aunt. "I want to keep one of your doily ornaments, if I may?"

And soon the large pile was distributed into smaller groups by each girl's place.

The craft box reappeared and the table, clean again, held dishes for the evening meal.

Beulah returned to her spot in the kitchen where she was assembling a shepherd's pie. All the days of visiting, Beulah and Sarah Marie were inseparable, talking recipes, cooking southern-fried chicken, and making breads.

"For my contribution to this Christmas dinner, I'm making an English Christmas bread pudding full of currants and gooseberries from your bushes. I'll make two, one for now and one for the real Christmas day. You can make the sauce when you want to eat it. The bread pudding I'll wrap in gauze and you can soak it in rum while you store it in your underground cellar. You'll have to put it inside a copper boiler with a tight lid, though, so the mice don't eat it."

Sarah Marie smiled. *I don't allow liquor in my house, but Beulah doesn't need to know that today.*

Beulah pointed to the stack of recipes she had been recording. The sauce recipe is here. It's mostly sugar and butter mixed 'til creamy."

Amelia sat back in the one comfortable chair that was reserved for Jack to rest in before bedtime. She picked up the book but did not open it. Instead, her mind wandered back over the events of the last weeks while visiting with her sister and her family.

Isn't it a shame we are so far away. I'd love to be able to spend time with all of them. Somehow, before I leave here, Sarah Marie and I will have a private talk. Maybe the girls can take turns coming to Virginia and attending college if they desire to do so.

If Joseph does settle out here, he can be their chaperone. Things can be arranged with a bit of creative planning. Mother and I rattle about in that big house.

Even though company was there, Sarah Marie went about doing her chores. She had tasks for her mother, and she kept Amelia busy in the early morning hours before the sun grew too hot to work outside weeding in the garden. Early afternoon found her with the girls shelling peas, scraping carrots and other vegetables to ready them for the evening meal.

Beulah made special meals which the men enjoyed. Southern cooking called for lard and lots of it. Fried vegetables that had been dipped in beaten eggs, rolled in herb flours melted in their mouths, and Beulah always made sure there were second servings for the men. Jack commented every night that he was going to have to punch new holes in his belt or get suspenders to hold his pants up.

Even though the group was cramped in the small house, there was plenty of love in their hearts and their mutual respect for each other made it an enjoyable time. Amelia felt a bit of nostalgia every evening at bedtime, realizing the day was approaching when they would be saying their goodbyes at the gate."

The minute Sarah Marie's feet hit the floor she was off and running the whole day. The daily chore list hung by the back screen door: Feed the chickens and turkeys, gather eggs, slop the pigs after each of our meals; sweep the kitchen floor, wash dishes, make your beds, make bread, separate the milk into cream, make butter. It was endless. One of the dirtiest jobs was cleaning the kerosene lamps.

Every day in the fall, she had the girls bring in the vegetables for canning. Hot steam filled the tiny kitchen as row upon row of filled Mason jars lined the counter top. The girls sang Sunday School songs in harmony while preparing the jars for the canning process.

The weekly chores included hand washing clothes, hanging out the clothes, retrieving dried clothes, folding and putting away those clothes in drawers. One important job was heating water for the large metal bathtub.

Chopping wood into kindling pieces was a tiresome job, but important come winter time. Killing chickens and plucking them for cooking and canning was another job. The laying hens were kept in the chicken house as Sarah Marie used eggs every day in her cooking and baking.

In the evenings, Sarah Marie was never without something in her hands. She knitted sweaters and mittens, darned socks and cut up flour sacks. During the winter she worked on quilt tops. The girls learned the craft right along with her. Sometimes neighbor women came for quilting bees. Sarah Marie would inspect their stitches and, if not to her satisfaction, she would rip them out, never telling the ladies of her doing so.

The flour sacks turned into new aprons, underwear, skirts and blouses for the girls and herself. She would pick the prettiest flour sack designs for outerwear, and the plain ones stitched up nicely into slips and panties. Her treadle sewing machine made a comfortable clickity-clack sound way into the night on many occasions. She knew too well the meaning of the phrase, "Burning the midnight oil." Sarah Marie's life was predictable and orderly.

How Sarah Marie accomplished all of these chores seemed magical to Amelia who had lived her entire life with a maid to keep her household running smoothly.

When was there time for fun projects like making root beer? Sarah Marie had her life in balance the same as Jack. She worked with the seasons, kept a clean house and had a system to her life. They were all healthy and happy.

The girls taught each other from books Sarah Marie had Amelia send every fall. They attended the public school when the weather allowed safe travels. At the end of May, the community held a pot luck supper at the school house. That was the day one of the local grandmother's took off her long underwear and proclaimed, "Spring has sprung." Awards for the children were passed out in front of proud parents.

Other events brought the community together, such as a wedding, and the Fourth of July. The women brought their best dishes, their aprons and their stored up gossip. The men who had instruments, played for several hours in the Stearn's Hall while their neighbors danced. Members of The Modern Woodsmen of America, a fraternal organization that Jack belonged to, volunteered their time and bodies to build the hall.

Thankfully, no accidents or major illnesses had befallen any of them, requiring a doctor's assistance. Sarah Marie knew a great deal about medicine and the use of herbs. She was called upon often to assist in setting a broken leg, human or animal, and she kept tinctures for dressing wounds, along with making a homemade concoction for the flu.

There was no church in the area for miles around. However, on occasion, a traveling minister, like Brother Van, would let it be known of his whereabouts and the neighbors would pass along the news. Camp meetings took place in the summertime and the Frey's attended when they could.

The room was quiet and Amelia was quite content with her thoughts. She did not hear her mother enter.

"Amelia, are you asleep?"

Startled, Amelia jumped in the comfortable chair. "Not really. I was wool gathering, I guess." She looked up to see her mother looking back.

"Jack wants his chair."

~34~

Time to Leave the Homestead

Joseph had never in his life been so tired and aching. He had a blister on one heel, blisters on two of his fingers. His eyes were sunburned and red. Mosquito bites and horsefly bites made welts on his face and arms where the insects had found a way to get under the clothes. Even with all the ailments, he was proud of what he had accomplished in the two weeks of working on the farm.

Every young man should come west and see for themselves what it is really all about to live out here in the arid landscape and eke out a living. I'll not purchase another Ned Buntline book filled with all that romantic redskin propaganda.

The first night after a day of hard work, Sarah Marie had a large bottle of liniment waiting for him on the kitchen table.

"Joseph here is some liniment for you to rub on your knees and shoulders. We put this on the horses. It stings a bit, but you'll be grateful when it heats up those inflamed bones." Joseph wasn't sure just what it was, but he accepted it eagerly.

Sarah Marie also set out a bottle with a skull and crossbones on the label. "This is Venetian Violet. We put it on everything like scratches, bug bites, anything that ails you." Joseph accepted her medicines and was eager to apply the fluid to his skin.

Little did he know the purple stain would remain for days on his face and when Joseph turned to look into a tin square, hanging for a mirror over the wash basin, he saw a purple polka-dotted nose, cheeks, and squinty eyes staring back.

"Oh, Joseph. I am so sorry. I forgot to tell you to use it sparingly. It stains deep into the skin and lasts forever. Your mark, say your own badge of courage, will be a reminder of this trip for a long time." She put her hand on her nephew's arm.

"This has been a wonderful time for me to finally get to see Mother once more." A tear formed on her eyelid but she held it back, blinking rapidly and smiling brightly. "I don't know when we will ever be able to come east, but one never knows what is in the future, do we?"

Joseph smiled at his Auntie Sarah Marie. "We will see to it that we are together more often, Auntie. The train ride is pleasant and not too expensive." He paused only for a moment. "Auntie, can you keep a secret?"

Sarah Marie's face lit up as she nodded the affirmative.

"I am very seriously falling in love with this place called the 'wild west' and there is a possibility I will move here maybe next year."

Sarah Marie put her hand over her mouth to stifle a gasp.

"I plan to make inquiry when we return to Helena in a couple of days. I think there is room for a surgeon who is interested in teaching medicine, having a private practice, and maybe even meeting the perfect bride?"

"That would be wonderful." Sarah Marie paused. "I understand your desires, as I wanted to come west my whole life. I know it looks like we have hard times and some years we do, but, all-in-all, I don't want to live anywhere else but where I'm planted now."

Amelia entered the room and felt the currents flowing between nephew and aunt.

"What are you two up to? Care to fill me in?"

"Nope."

Joseph reached for a dipper full of water from the bucket, Sarah Marie walked to the Hoosier pie cabinet, and Amelia just stood there with her mouth open.

Joseph chuckled as he turned to show his mother his purple spots.

"How do you like my makeup, Mother? Auntie fixed me up real good. Nothing aches, or itches, or burns, or creaks. This stuff works like a charm. Do we have it in the barn at home? I think we need it for our patients, too." He laughed. "We were taught in medical school that this stuff was just snake oil, sold by fast-talking salesmen. You know . . . the cure all stuff in the dark brown bottle with a cork in it?"

Amelia picked up the small bottle with the skull and cross bones. She read the label and was amazed that her son so willingly had applied the liquid to his skin. She kept her tongue, but shook her head.

The sun was not yet up, but the breakfast meal had been prepared and served. Their early morning rise gave the travelers more cool air for traveling back to Helena. Jack and Jackie had the team hitched, the little tag-along wagon secured behind, and it was time for the goodbye hugs. The men were nervous about the tears that surely were to flow within a few minutes.

"Goodbye, my daughter. It has been a real adventure and education to see how you live happily with your husband and family." Mrs. Roberts held her baby girl much too tightly, then abruptly pulled away and put her hand into Joseph's for help climbing into the buggy. She looked so sad, that Joseph thought maybe her heart would break.

Next came Beulah and she gave a farewell hug to her forever friend. She shook Jackie's and Jack's hands, and kissed each girl on the cheek. Without a word she also entered into the confines of the black buggy.

Now Amelia could put it off no longer. She put her arms around her sister's shoulders and did not stop her tears from flowing onto the collar of her dress.

"Goodbye once again, little sister. Please remember our conversation from last night. Mother and I will be sending you some inheritance from Father's estate."

She gave a quick hug to each of the girls. "Every one of you is welcome to move back to Virginia to attend college, live with me, take some trips. Plan to see Europe." She stopped and looked to the sky. "No more lost time because of distance must pass between us. We are family." Amelia accepted Joseph's arm and he helped her find her seat.

"Thank you Uncle Jack and Auntie. You have taught me so much." He winked at his aunt. "Be seeing you." They hugged each other and Sarah Marie planted a kiss on Joseph's purple cheek. She whispered in his ear, "Parting is such sweet sorrow."

With that, Joseph hopped into the buggy and gave a snap of the reins. The horses flinched, lazy from having nothing to do but eat green grass in the meadow for over fourteen days. But once they made their first steps, they were eager to be on the trail. One stomped his front hoof and leaned into the harness.

The Frey family stood by the huge wooden pole gate and waved as the buggy and trailer went through. Jackie swung it shut, dropped the wire latch and shouted one more goodbye as the horses picked up speed going down the dirt lane.

Goodbye, goodbye, all of you, goodbye. Sarah Marie stood there, tears flowing. She remained as if she had been turned to stone, with her right arm in the air, her hand holding a wet and crumpled white cotton handkerchief.

A sad goodbye

~35~

Cowboy Funeral

It was a welcome sight for the bone-tired travelers when Wolf Creek came into view. The buggy had springs for comfort, but even so, the heat of the day had to have been near 100 degrees.

Their many overlays of clothing were cumbersome for the women, and Amelia wished she had not worn all the layers. Umbrellas, hand fans, and canvas water canteens kept the four people from fainting in the buggy from sheer exhaustion. Even with the weather so beastly hot, no one complained.

Joseph stopped occasionally and gave the two horses water whenever a group of shade trees appeared on the trail. It was on one such stop that they noticed a group of cowboys following behind a funeral procession.

Beulah spotted the riderless horse. The animal's mane and tail had been brushed and the hide combed until the animal glowed in the sunlight. The beautiful, rather ornate roping saddle was empty. A leather bridle, with chunks of silver and turquoise, had a lead rope threaded through the attached ring on the casket wagon.

Beulah and Mrs. Roberts, Amelia and Joseph, all stood at attention as the caparisoned horse paraded by.

"Look, Mother. The boots are reversed in the stirrups and pointed backwards." Amelia pointed her index finger in the direction of the riderless horse.

"So it is. The first time I saw that in a procession was for our slain president, Abraham Lincoln." Mrs. Roberts put her hand over her heart. "The dead cowboy is riding backwards, looking to see who had come to bury him." She smiled at Joseph. "I know that probably seems strange to you, son, but in Lincoln's time, it was an honor for the generals and high officers to be recognized as leaders of their troops. They were given one last chance to oversee their units by riding backwards."

"I've read about this, Grandmother. It seems the idea goes clear back to Ghingus Kahn and his funeral procession." Joseph held tightly to the reins of his rented horses. He didn't want them spooked by the passing cortege.

"In those days they would put the body in the ground, then kill his horse and bury it with him so he would have a horse to ride as a warrior in the next life." Joseph smiled at his mother. "This cowboy's funeral tells us he was a respected man."

Amelia's thoughts were thousands of miles away. *I remember during the Civil War how the surviving men from a battle would take off the clothes of the dead man so they could have shoes. A supply wagon team would drag the dead horses off the field to be used for food. No one worried about who the poor fellow was; some had their name and where they were from written on a piece of paper carried in their shirt pockets, but most of the men did not. I guess they thought it was a sign of bad luck or something.*

"Apparently this man is going to be buried on his ranch. I don't see a community cemetery anywhere close." Amelia shielded her eyes from the bright sunlight. A cowboy, playing *"Oh! Bury Me Not On The Lone Prairie . . ."* on his harmonica, accompanied the procession. The parade drifted off to the left, out of sight of the buggy. Not a word or a wave had passed between the two parties.

"We best be on our way in to Wolf Creek," said Joseph. Amelia and Beulah helped Mrs. Roberts back into the buggy, and then they took turns stepping inside.

Tilda saw them coming and she waved a large American flag at them. "Whoa!" shouted Joseph. He pulled up to the post office building and saluted Tilda. He raised his right hand to his hat brim in a salute to the flag. "Hello, Tilda. Have you been waiting all day for us?"

"Yep."

Tilda turned and ran up the steps.

"Mama, they're here. Come quick."

"Josie greeted them with a smile and a welcoming hand. "Your rooms are the same and waiting for you. But first, come inside. Tilda and I have spring water and tea, and I can make a pot of coffee if anyone wants that. You all look rather beat." She motioned with her hand for them to follow her up the steps and onto the shaded porch where wicker rockers tempted them.

"I want to hear all about the things you did at the homestead with Sarah Marie and the girls and Jackie. Did Jack get Joseph out into the fields?" She looked at Joseph and saw his purple spots. "My goodness, yes, he did. You are as black as Beulah, young man."

"Laws, Josie, I've been telling them we is 'kin' for nigh on to 45 years now." Beulah crossed her arms covering her bosom front. Everybody had a good laugh.

"Josie, we stopped for a funeral procession outside of town. Was that a local farmer?" asked Joseph.

"No," answered Josie. "That group of cowboys is from over Helmville way. The dead man was John Keiley. He and his brother had an understanding that whoever died first, the other brother would come fetch the body and take it home for a place to rest in peace. I heard they have been far north of here, and have been travelling for several days. One of my customers came for mail the other day, and told me that they would pack the body in the coffin in dirt to keep it from decaying in this heat." She counted on her fingers. "They should reach their destination by the end of this week. They will cut through here, and make it to Marysville, for camp night, then across to Elliston and Avon, and then one more day to their last stop, Helmville. The cowboys are from the Keiley ranch."

The evening passed quietly. The next morning found the group on their last lap to Helena, where a hotel full of luxuries awaited.

~36~

Joseph Reveals His Plans

Sunlight filled Joseph's room as he sat in the wing-tipped maroon chair facing the lace covered windows. To his surprise, people were already milling about, even though it was barely sunrise. He watched shopkeepers opening their store fronts, sweeping off the stoops from the dust that had settled overnight. The clank of milk wagons and delivery wagons seemed like a song as they took turns stopping at various doors with their fresh products and wares.

I am in love with this town. Joseph pulled back one of the curtain panels for a better view and he watched people in the park across the courtyard from the hotel. A train pulled slowly into the area.

I can understand mother's returning to Virginia, I guess, so that I could be well educated, but the future of our country lies here in the west. I want to be a part of that. How am I going to tell her I plan to return here? Will she understand and be happy for me? Maybe even move back here with me? Joseph walked the floor. *No, she won't leave her mother even with her two brothers close by. Her place is with Grandmother.*

He heard a tap-tap on his door.

"Yes?" he answered. "I'm awake and dressed." He smiled as he pulled open the door. "Surprise! I've been out for a walk already, Mother."

Amelia jumped back when the door swung open. "We are going downstairs for breakfast. Just so you know where to find us."

Joseph stepped into the hall. "Mother, you seem sad this morning. Are you?" He put his long arm across his mother's shoulders and gave her a hug. "It has been a wonderful time visiting for you and Beulah and Grandmother, hasn't it? Visiting Auntie Sarah Marie and seeing how she lives, and . . . ."

Amelia cut him short. "Let's not talk about that here in the hallway, son. I'll be downstairs." She looked straight into his bright blue eyes. "You look so much like your father." She turned on her high-heeled shoe and left Joseph standing at his door.

The bellhops, in their maroon jackets and black pants with gold braiding, moved quickly to place the bags onto wheeled carts. A dumbwaiter at the end of the long hallway saved them from hand-carrying the heavy baggage to the street level of the hotel. It took several trips to empty out the rooms, but they were finished with everything except the carry-on luggage that Amelia, Beulah and Mrs. Roberts would be taking onto the train. Joseph had a carpetbag for his shaving equipment and clothes.

The heavy luggage would be put into a freight car, and he hoped it would arrive at their destination. They would be riding the train for a week. They had sleeping rooms. Beulah would bunk in with Amelia. Their plans were to spend two days in Chicago, visiting family friends and touring that wonderful city.

Time stood still and yet the leaving hour arrived much too quickly. The bills were paid for the rental of the horses and buggy and the stable fees. The Broadwater Hotel bill was paid with money that Amelia had made in exchange for her Virginia greenbacks as promised.

Everyone was shifting gears, preparing for the long ride in the drafty passenger train. Amelia planned to spend most of her time in the dining car where she could enjoy the passing terrain and gaze at the Rocky Mountains. Joseph planned to write in his journal about this amazing adventure.

Beulah and Amelia were both lost in their own unspoken thoughts as they waited for the elder woman to board with Joseph's help. The two couldn't help but wipe away an escaped tear, both knowing they would never be this way again. They had said their goodbyes to Sarah Marie, shedding tears openly as they left the homestead.

"Montana in the fall season has to be the prettiest state in our United States," said Joseph. "The trees and bushes just overnight look like Jack Frost visited them . . . just look up at that sapphire blue sky with fluffy white clouds . . . it is almost more than the eye can take in one setting." He sat deep in the dining car chair, enjoying a cup of tea and some cookies that one of the waiters had set out for them to nibble on.

Amelia broke the silence that was developing between them.

"We have certainly seen distinct weather patterns almost overnight, that is for sure. Why, I'll never forget watching you help your Uncle Jack with cutting the hay. You looked so happy behind that team of horses bucking up the hay from the long furrows you had made the day before." Amelia smiled, waiting, anticipating her son to speak.

"It was hard work, I'll tell you, Mother. But yes, I did enjoy all the daily activities of farm life. My goodness, it is no wonder Auntie Sarah Marie is rail thin. She just goes the minute her feet hit that pine wood floor in the morning and I'll bet you she never sleeps a deep sleep because she has so much on her list of chores to do each day."

He bit into another cookie. "These are very good; crispy the way Beulah makes them." Joseph put his arms on the table top and folded his hands.

"Mother, we are alone and I think it is time to talk to you about something."

Amelia returned her hands to her lap.

The train click-clacked on down the rails.

"Remember a couple of days ago when I went for a long walk by myself?"

I wanted some time alone to think about all I had seen, heard, and done while on this trip."

Amelia nodded her head, but said nothing.

"While on that walk I came upon a private college that is being built on the hill on the north edge of town.

You know where I mean." He paused and looked at Amelia's face.

She knows what I am going to tell her. I don't want to break her heart, but I have to make my own decisions about my life. Well, here goes. Please God, give me the right words on a blessed tongue.

"Mother, I stopped at the building site and found the contractor, who in turn, told me who to contact about employment as a professor of medicine. I made the connection within the hour. I wrote out my resume. Possibly there will be a position for me when the building is complete, probably a year from now. It is to be a male-only institution with emphases on medicine, sciences, religion, mathematics, Latin, languages, and . . . ." Joseph stopped talking in mid-sentence. His mother had reached out her hand and placed it on top of his.

Amelia squeezed her eyes tight. *This is no time for tears. He must not see me distressed. I felt this conversation coming when we were in the cemetery. Now, I must let him make his own way.* Amelia looked straight into her son's bright blue eyes.

"You are a very fine doctor with modern learning and techniques, just what this town needs. *You* will be the doctor I tried to be. *You* will make great strides in the health and well-being of a town that still remembers the name of Dr. A. Martin, M. D." Amelia dropped her eyes. "Promise me you will visit me and not wait twenty five years to come back to your family."

Joseph felt the piercing of her heart at that very moment. In reality, she was still very active with her medical skills. She kept up with the latest equipment and even attended conventions on occasion, meeting other female doctors who continued to fight the battle of "no women doctors."

Now that he had brought his secret to the forefront, he knew she would accept and embrace his decision wholeheartedly. This next year would mean extra schooling for him, as well as fulfilling his dream of someday being a professor of medicine.

For Amelia the train ride became a torture as she continued to think about the news Joseph had shared with her. The life of sacrifice had always been one for her to live, beginning as a teenage girl working alongside of her mother who acted as a nurse, aiding her doctor father. She had attended medical school against all odds of graduating. One of the hardest to bear was losing her husband within just a few months of their marriage. Deciding to run away from the familiar in her grief, then delivering her baby in a small town in a western territory should have been enough, but more followed.

Amelia recalled her beginning days as a doctor in Helena, Montana Territory and the struggles of health care and surgeries in a mining town full of horrible and tragic accidents. She fought flu epidemics, burying more children than she saved.

She knew her presence in Helena was important, but other doctors had also arrived in the area, and Amelia recognized her own child's needs. She returned to Virginia, knowing that her late husband would want his son educated at Harvard. Although she had suitors over the years, marriage never interested her as she led a busy life in her community.

Amelia looked out the train window but did not see the large herd of cattle standing near the fence as the train rumbled by. Too lost in her thoughts, all she could focus on was her tenacity and the passing of her lifetime.

Joseph has formed a decision and spoken of it out loud. So be it. She listened to the monotonous clickety-clack of the wheels on the iron rails. *Trains go in both directions. We'll be in contact. Life will reveal its plan for my son. He'll meet a nice, frontier woman whose parents pioneered the west and helped discover this town just like I planned to do. He'll find love and build a home; he'll be a wonderful professor of medicine, and his name will be linked forever to the history of the college.*

This time, as tears spilled down her cheeks, she did not try to stop them.

Oh! Life is always so full of surprises. I never thought Joseph would fall in love with his birthplace, but I do understand. Even for me, just seeing it again has made me wish for other things for myself as well. I will make this coming year special for all of us, and I will not mope around. My decision was made years ago. Mother needs attention now. She won't admit that to anyone, however.

This is Joseph's time to reach out for new beginnings . . . and there is definitely no time for tears.

A Mother holds her children's hands

for a while . . .

their hearts forever.
Author Unknown

Mr. and Mrs. Frey celebrating their
50th wedding anniversary

Author's Notes

Sarah Marie and Jack Frey lived on the homestead for over 60 years, semi-retiring, but never too far away from their land and children. She instilled the love of life into her children.

Helen, Jackie's mother, died in childbirth.

Celine, educated at several universities throughout the country, taught school in California, Chicago, and Montana. Celine married but did not have any children. She travelled extensively throughout the world and retired in Mexico.

Elsie moved to Idaho, married, raised a large family, and became a successful business woman, owning a resort.

Gertrude married a farmer in Montana. She was left a widow as a very young woman. She later married a scientist and they both worked for the United States Navy in California. They travelled the world both professionally and as tourists.

The baby daughter, Nora Bee, graduated from Helena High School, married Thomas A. McKelvey. They raised five children, Ellen, Jimmie, Sheila, Lenore and Patrick. Nora Bee worked as a secretary for the State of Montana Highway Department while Thomas served in the Army during World War II. Upon his return, they built a paint and art store business in Helena, Montana. Nora Bee loved to travel. As a child, she thought the mountain tops surrounding the ranch held up the sky. She saw her first airplane and stood spellbound as it disappeared from her sight. She wanted to find out where that plane went. Nora Bee owned the Frey homestead until her death.

Jack (Jackie) Severtson, Helen's son, and the Frey's grandson, stayed on the homestead and built up a cattle herd. He retired from ranching and worked as a mechanic for many years in the Great Falls, Montana area. He lives in Great Falls, Montana with his wife, Bess. He has two grown children and many grandchildren.

Nora Bee's oldest daughter, Ellen, continues to run the Frey homestead along with her four sons, grandchildren and great grandchildren.

The Hicks family continues to ranch in the Helena area. Matilda "Tilda" aka "Tillie" Hicks married John Murphy. She also was the post mistress in Wolf Creek, Montana for many years. Tillie was the mother of Earl Murphy who married Ellen McKelvey. Thus the circle remains unbroken for these two families portrayed in *No Time for Tears.*

This book has been complicated to write because of all the connections throughout the 150+ years of life for these two families. I wrote from recorded history, letters, genealogy, records kept in old Bibles, and stories passed down from family to family.

My purpose was to portray an ordinary group of people, living what would be considered an ordinary lifestyle for the times they lived in. However, the more I researched, the more it became clear that these women were far from ordinary. They sought life and adventure. They followed their dreams and made a difference in the lives of others who came into and along that path with them.

I, Lenore McKelvey Puhek, granddaughter of Mary and Jack Frey, will remain forever grateful for their DNA that lingers in me, giving me the spark and curiosity to be looking around the next corner I come to. From them I learned value of reading, writing, exploring, travelling, questioning and wondering about the world around me.

Most of all, I want to thank God for blessing me with the gift of writing.

About the Author

Lenore McKelvey Puhek holds a BA in English/Writing from Carroll College, Helena, Montana. This is her fourth book in the award winning series of writing about pioneer women who did not receive the limelight during their lifetime. Puhek is a member of the Western Writers of America, Montana Historical Society, State of Montana Cowboy and Western Heritage Center Hall of Fame, and other writing groups. She is available for public speaking.

Contact: E-mail: lpuhek@gmail.com

The author, age two months, hanging on tight to her
Grandfather Frey's finger

CPSIA information can be obtained at www.ICGtesting.com
Printed in the USA
BVOW01s0317231013

334387BV00003B/3/P

9 781491 707777